Second Chance Baby

AXEL AND CHASTITY

BOOK FIVE

LEXIE MIERS

CHAPTER 1

Patrick

I woke up on a perfect Sunday morning with my beautiful, pregnant woman in my arms. Smiling, I kissed her head, listening to the sound of her light snores.

She was fast asleep, which was great. She needed the rest.

When I'd gone to pick her up yesterday from Chastity's school, Axel had called me. I sighed against Kaiti's hair as I recalled the conversation. The phone had rung, and I'd put it on loudspeaker immediately, ready for a fight...

"I was just about to call you," I said.

Axel's chuckle filled the car. "Chastity asked me to give her some time to speak to you. Did she call?" he asked casually.

"Uh, yeah, she did," I answered, which he'd already known, or he wouldn't have been calling me in the first place.

"So, is everything okay with you two?" he went on.

I clenched my jaw tight and exhaled steadily through my nose. "Yeah, she and I are fine. You and me, on the other hand..."

Are not okay. Very not okay.

"I wanted to tell you weeks ago, Pat, but Chastity asked me not to," Axel rushed in to say. "She said she wanted to be the one to tell you."

I nodded even though I knew he couldn't see me, but my jaw was clenched so tightly, I couldn't verbally respond.

Axel continued even though I didn't want him to. "I love her, Pat, and I'm *really* excited about the baby. I hope you can be happy for us, too."

I wasn't happy for anyone, least of all the man I'd once considered my best friend. But instead of shooting him straight down, I managed to grate out, "You're going to need to give me some time, Axel."

"For what?" he demanded. "I told you I love her, that I'll take care of her. I'd marry her if she wanted. If this was any other woman, you'd be happy for me. In fact, you'd probably say something like, 'Shit, this woman must be pretty amazing if you want to commit like that. Wow. You're going to be a dad. I never thought I'd see the day!"

I couldn't stop the laugh that bubbled up. He was one hundred percent right. If he'd gotten anyone else pregnant, I would have slapped him on the back and bought him a bottle of bourbon. But *my* daughter...? "You're an asshole."

"Come on, man. Can't you separate the two for just a minute?"

I kept one hand on the wheel and scrubbed the other through my hair in frustration. "I can try," I offered.

I honestly had no idea if I was ever going to feel comfortable with Axel being with Chastity. But did I have a choice? Not really, not if I didn't want to lose my daughter.

"Fine," Axel huffed in response. "Hey, Pat, guess what? I'm going to be a father!"

I swallowed hard. *Okay... let's try this again.* "Congrats, buddy," I said, though even to my ears my tone was strained. "When's she due?" I pressed ahead, giving this my best shot.

"Early October," he answered brightly.

He knows the due date? At least that was something. He forgot some of his ex-girlfriends' names half the time.

"Any news on your end?" Axel asked suddenly. "You know, with that woman you started seeing, and I didn't tell Chastity about?" Axel coughed to drive home the point.

I rolled my eyes. *Yeah, yeah, okay.* He'd done me a solid favor there. "Yeah, actually. I didn't think it would last past the first few dates, but it's ended up being good."

"With your ex? That's surprising."

Yes, it was more than a little surprising for me too. I laughed. "Yeah, it has been. We... well, both of us have changed and grown a lot. But anyway, I have news of my own too."

"Tell me," Axel encouraged, just like he would any other day. Like he didn't already know.

I sighed, realizing that I hadn't told anyone this news yet. Axel would be my first. "Kaiti's pregnant. I'm going to be a father again."

"I want to say congratulations," Axel said cautiously. "But you don't sound very happy about it."

I groaned in response, a shift happening within me that allowed me to be honest, the way I had always been with my closest friend. "Well, I —well... look. I *am* happy. It's just very unexpected."

Axel laughed, genuine humor in his voice. "Is it too early to make a joke about the fact you've only managed to knock up a woman twice, and it was the same woman twenty-two years apart?"

If I hadn't been driving, I would have slapped myself in the head. It'd occurred to me too, and I'd found it punch-me-in-the-face ironic as well. "Yeah, go for it," I said. "I've thought it myself a few times already."

"You two've obviously got good chemistry. What were the odds of her getting pregnant again?"

"At forty-three?" I asked, a snort escaping me. "The doctor said about one or two percent."

"Whoa. Sounds like fate to me, Pat."

I groaned. "You sound like Chastity. Stop it." I didn't want anything pointing out just how well-suited they were. Not even now.

"Hey, listen. I'm on my way to see Chastity right now. I need to suck up for a mistake I made on Wednesday," Axel said. "Can we catch up tomorrow, maybe? Dinner on me?"

I glared through the windshield. He'd managed to upset my pregnant daughter already? *For fuck's sake.* "Do I want to know what you did wrong?"

"I missed her sonogram because I had to take some work calls," he admitted.

I laughed. I couldn't help it. *Fuckwit.* "I knew it! Your job is going to get in the way of you two."

Axel was a player, that much had always been true, but he was a workaholic first and foremost. It was the reason he'd never committed to a woman in the past. He just didn't have time. His business was his life. *It* was his baby.

"Shut up. I'm trying to fix it, okay?" he snarked right back.

I'll believe it when I see it. "Yeah, right. But okay, dinner tomorrow. I'll meet you at Jack's at eight?" Chastity was upset with me too. I might as well try to do something to mend the rift; a bit of damage control for how her mother and I reacted to her own baby news.

"Yeah. Perfect. See you then."

After Axel had hung up, I'd picked Kaiti up and brought her home. I'd focused on her from that moment, but now I had to deal with the fact that I had dinner at Jack's tonight with Axel; a man I still seriously wanted to punch in the face. I couldn't believe he'd fallen for my daughter *and* gotten her pregnant almost immediately. It was just... so... unlike Axel.

"Good morning," Kaiti groaned out, rolling onto her back to stare up at me. "How long have you been up?"

I shrugged. "Not long, beautiful. I've just been enjoying holding you."

Her eyes opened wide, as though she didn't believe I'd actually said that.

It wasn't an unusual response. After almost twenty years apart and playing out the roles of exes, I understood that she was shocked whenever I said something nice. "How are you feeling this morning, anyway?" I asked, lifting my hand to move her hair back off her face.

She swallowed and gulped a little. "Not great," she breathed. "Actually, excuse me." She rolled out of bed as fast as she was able and bolted for the ensuite. The sounds of retching soon filled the bathroom.

I got up to get her a bottle of water from the kitchen.

When I got back to the bedroom, she was sitting on the toilet, urinating, pale as a sheet.

"Here you go." I handed her the bottle of water and gave her some privacy.

Being a Sunday morning, the last thing I wanted to do was rush off. So, I went back to the kitchen and cut up some fruit, plated it up and brought it back to the bed with me.

Kaiti opened the door to ensuite and practically crawled back beneath the covers.

"Strawberries?" I asked, offering the plate.

She buried her face into the pillow a little more. "No thank you, hon."

I set the plate aside and lay down with her again. Her hair was so thick and beautiful. I could never stop myself from running my fingers through it.

"Do you have any plans today?" Kaiti asked, her voice muffled by the pillow somewhat.

I froze. *Should I tell her about my meet up with Axel?* "Ah... why do you ask?"

She didn't even lift her head. "I don't think I'm getting up much today. So, if you need to go to the gym or anything, it's okay. Please. I just want to rest."

I smiled and pressed a kiss to her forehead. "I have dinner plans with a colleague, but nothing else planned. I can help you today if you like?"

She rolled over and nestled into me, wiggling her butt into my groin. "Can we just cuddle for a while?"

With a contented smile I slid my hand over her waist and pressed my palm to her still flat belly. "Of course. Just you and me and bub."

Her breath hitched in her throat, but she didn't say anything.

I closed my eyes and held her tightly. "I love you, Kaiti. I always have."

"And I love you," she whispered back.

We stayed like that for most of the day, talking, cuddling, and eating in bed.

Around 7:30 PM I took a shower, got changed, and headed off to Jack's. Part of me felt guilty about not telling Kaiti that I was seeing Axel, but I also felt like I had to deal with my own feelings toward him. Our friendship was strained to the point of no return, and if my daughter really had chosen him to be her *forever*, then I owed them both the chance to fix it.

Axel was already there, seated in the back, wine ordered and on the table. He stood up as I entered the restaurant and held out his hand.

I reached out and shook it, even though my gut churned with anger.

"Thanks for coming, buddy," he said. "Do you want to order right away?" Axel signaled the waiter.

I nodded and sat down, ordering a rare steak while pouring myself a glass of the red Axel had waiting.

"Does Kaiti know you're here?" Axel asked, taking a sip of his wine.

I shook my head. "Nope. How about Chastity?" I asked in return.

Axel laughed. "Nope."

Good. At least we were on the same wavelength.

"So," Axel began. "We're going to wind up with kids pretty much the same age. Can't say I ever would have thought *that* was going to happen."

I snorted. "And I never thought I'd have a grandchild who'd be older than my own kid, but *that's* happening."

Axel's eyes widened, then his mouth dropped open. "Whoa, yeah. I hadn't thought about that."

I grimaced. "I have, and it's kind of fucked up." Our dinner arrived and I tucked into my steak, having not eaten much for the day but small portions of snack food—basically whatever Kaiti could keep down. "How's work?" I asked, and we chatted like normal for a while. Just shit about the market and finances, the gym and working out. But after another glass of wine, I decided to get more serious. "So? Is there anything else you want to say to me? You were the one that called this dinner, after all."

Axel leaned back into his chair and nodded. "Yeah. I wanted you to know how serious I am about making this work with Chastity. I've already hired one manager, and I intend to hire at least three more to help lift the load off my shoulders."

My jaw would have literally dropped off if I wasn't interrogating him. "You're going to delegate?" I asked in shock. "Yeah, right."

He shrugged. "I've already started."

Hm... "You seriously want me to believe you're a changed man?"

Axel grinned at me. "You can believe whatever you want, Patrick. You know I'll fuck up along the way, but my goal now is to be the father

I never had. I want to be there for my kid. Be present... or, hell, what-ever. I don't want to be at work wondering what's going on at home."

I nodded slowly, taking another sip of my wine. "You've really thought about this, haven't you?"

He stared at me, his eyes alight with determination. "I never meant to fall in love with her, Pat; but I am set on doing this right."

"But you meant to get her pregnant?" I asked, determined to know.

The side of Axel's lips pinched. "I didn't intentionally get her pregnant, but I didn't exactly prevent it."

"So, it *was* intentional." I couldn't help but smirk. I'd been right. "Better than her trapping your ass, I guess?"

Axel chuckled. "Yeah, if you want to put it that way. So... does this mean we can be friends again, Pat?" he asked hopefully.

I sighed and checked my phone.

Kaiti was messaging to say goodnight.

"I want to. But let's just take it a week at a time, yeah?"

Kaiti wasn't going to be so quick to forgive and forget, I knew that for sure and certain.

Axel nodded and threw some cash on the check. "Fine by me. I just want you to know how much I'm trying to change."

"Just keep me in the loop in regard to Chastity, yeah?" I told him. "She's mad at me too at the moment, but if anything happens to her or... you know. You'll call me, right?"

Axel nodded. "Of course." He didn't mention anything about Chastity and my fight over dinner, which could only mean he already knew everything.

With effort, I changed the topic to football and let the rest of the night melt away in a casual blur of small talk and red wine. I wasn't sure where this friendship would ultimately go. Back to where it was, or in a totally new direction? But I wouldn't lose my daughter, so if that meant I had to make nice with Axel, I would.

I'll do anything to have my family back together again.

CHAPTER 2

Patrick

The next two weeks were rough on Kaiti. Her blood pressure was too high, and her morning sickness wasn't limited to the morning. She was sick all day and through the night. And even more concerning, her weight was dropping.

I was at work when she called me, and I answered immediately. "Hey beautiful, how was the doctor visit?"

She groaned, obviously annoyed. "He wants me to stop working!" she complained. "Like I can do that!" She hadn't been into work much in the last few weeks anyway, but I knew she had planned to return.

"You know you don't need to work," I said gently. "We looked at our finances on Sunday, remember? If we rent my place out, we can easily afford for you to stay home without stress."

Kaiti grumbled. "Yeah, but I don't want you having to pay for everything."

I tried not to laugh. She was so damn stubborn. "Kaiti, our baby is the only important thing here. If the doctor thinks you and our bub are better off at home, then why shouldn't we listen?" I spent most of my time at Kaiti's place, anyway. It wouldn't take much to put my furniture into storage and move in there permanently. Or at least until we could afford to get a bigger place of our own.

"Yeah, I suppose," she agreed, though she certainly didn't sound happy about it.

"Any other news?" I asked. "How's everything going with the pregnancy?"

"The baby's doing well, or so the doctor says," she grumbled.

"And your weight loss?" I asked anxiously.

"It's all within normal ranges given my GD, he assures me."

I wasn't so sure about that myself, but I was also hoping that once she felt better, she'd start eating better again. "Okay. Well, how about Thai or Chinese tonight?"

"Whatever you prefer," she answered. "You know I can't keep much down at the moment."

She sounded so sad and exhausted. This pregnancy was taking so much more out of her than her first one had—but then, she'd been twenty years younger back then. "Are you okay to get yourself home?"

"Yeah... I took an Uber."

My chest tightened but I forced myself to say, "Good girl. I'll see you in a few hours, okay?"

"Okay. Bye."

Since the weekend she'd seen Chastity and hadn't been able to drive home, Kaiti really hadn't done a lot more than drive to the local grocery store on occassion. I was grateful she was being smart about her well-being given our precious bundle, but for someone who was so fiercely independent, it scared me that she'd made that choice so easily. It meant that she was putting on a brave face and was even more fragile than I realized.

When my phone rang again, I grabbed for it, assuming it was Kaiti once more; But instead, it was my first born. "Chastity! How are you?" We hadn't spoken since she'd basically hung up on me. "Are you okay?" I asked, worried something might be wrong.

"Yeah, Dad. I'm great, actually. I miss you guys, though."

I grinned, the tightness in my chest eased with tangible relief. "We miss you too, sweetheart. How's college going and how's your morning sickness treating you?"

She chuckled. "Now, those are two questions I never dreamed you'd ask me in the same sentence."

I groaned, running my hand through my hair. "Well, me neither, if I'm being honest."

"Well, school is super. Finals are coming up shortly, but I'm on top of things, so it's all good. And I'm not suffering from any more sickness, thank God! That was really kicking my ass for a while there."

I nodded and hummed agreement but didn't tell Chastity how her mom was fairing, even though I wanted to. Something told me that Kaiti wouldn't want me to share. "That's wonderful, sweetie. Now, is there anything I can do for you? Or are you just calling to catch up?"

"Actually, I was kind of wondering if we could have dinner this weekend?" she asked. "I'm coming into the city, and Axel and I thought it would be nice to break the tension."

My jaw dropped and I suppressed the shudder that arose at the idea of going on a double date with my daughter and her boyfriend—who just so happened to be my best friend.

"Uh…" What could I say? I missed my daughter, and I knew Kaiti did deep down too. "Let me just double check with your mom on which night suits, but we'd love to."

"Oh. Great." Chastity sighed as though she was relieved. "I'll text you on Friday to confirm, but thanks, Dad. I really want to try and get back to where we were."

"Yeah, I do too, kiddo. Thanks for calling." I hung up with a strange sense of brewing anxiety in my chest. Dinner with the two of them was going to be as confrontational as hell. But it would also be the first time Chastity had seen her mother and me back together as well, so… yeah. This was definitely going to be a baptism by fire.

When I got home to Kaiti's house, she was pale and wan, lying in bed again. I was actually worried about her mental health now, not just the physical side of things. Instead of ordering in, I made a quick dinner and managed to get her to drink a fruit smoothie.

"Thank you," she said, handing me back the glass once she'd finished the heavily nutritious drink.

I sat down on the bed with her and reached for her hand. "So, have you given any thought to what I said about me moving in here full time?

She nodded, staring down at our entangled hands. "Yes," she admitted. "And although I *hate* the idea of relying on you for money like that, Patrick, you're right. The baby is more important than my pride."

I tugged her into my arms and wrapped her up, holding her tightly. "Thank God," I breathed. "I'm so relieved, beautiful. You know money means nothing. Nothing at all. You and your health, the baby's health... that's everything. It's all I care about."

She lifted her head with a fragile smile.

I leaned in gently and kissed her mouth, tasting the mango flavor on her lips from the smoothie. "How about a bath?" I asked, kissing her nose. "I can run it for you."

Kaiti's bathroom was tiny, as were most of the things in her house. One day, when we had a large family home, we'd have a bathtub big enough for both of us.

"That would be amazing, Patrick, thank you," she whispered, tears in her eyes.

I smiled and kissed her once more before pulling away to slip into her ensuite to get the water running. Kaiti was always teary nowadays and although I wanted to ask her if she was okay, I knew better than to enquire. Being pregnant at her age was a lot to process and the hormonal shifts—I could only imagine—were brutal.

I put the plug in and adjusted the water temperature after turning on the tap, before adding her favorite scented bubble bath. When I turned around, she was standing in the doorway naked, with her hair down and flowing over her shoulders.

She stared down at her feet and ran her hands self-consciously over her belly. "I'm already changing," she said.

In truth, she was thinner than when we'd begun to date again, but she'd always be beautiful in my eyes. "You're perfect, Kaiti. Look how dark your nipples are. Delicious."

Her head came up and she laughed. "I'm glad you think so."

"I absolutely do," I assured her. "And when you start feeling better, I'm going to prove it to you."

A heated blush blossomed on her cheeks as she scooped her long hair up and twisted it into a bun on top of her head. "You're just teasing me."

I laughed and reached for her. "Want me to prove to you right *now* how much I want you?"

She swatted my hands away and climbed into the bubble bath with a smile, her full breasts swinging in front of my eyes.

Definitely delicious.

"Do you want to stay and chat with me?" she asked hopefully as I turned to leave.

The room was filling with steam and her soft sigh made my heart wrench. "I'd love to." I sat down on the tiled floor and leaned back against the cool wall. "God, you're beautiful, Kaiti."

She scooped some water up to wash her face, blinking at me like an owl as she cleared her eyes. "Patrick, you're being too perfect. Please stop."

I huffed out a laugh. "Why?"

"Because I feel like crap, and I can't take you to bed and ravish you like I should." She leaned back with a relaxed sigh and her nipples peeked through the bubbles, catching my eye.

Damn it, now I was getting hard. *Time to change the subject.* "Okay... well, since you're being a cruel taskmistress and I can't tell you how much I love you *or* desire you, how about I settle for telling you about my day?"

She rested her head back against the edge of the bathtub. "Yes, please."

"Work was, you know, easy and boring; but at least it pays the bills."

She nodded, still staring at me. "Anything else?"

"Uh, yeah. Chastity called, actually."

That got her sitting up, the water sloshing up and down in the tub. "How come? What did she say?" she asked immediately.

"She wants us to meet her and Axel for dinner over the weekend."

Kaiti's eyebrows drew into a tight frown within two seconds flat. "And what did you say?" she asked warily.

"I said that I'd have to check in with you regarding which night suited best, but that we'd probably love to."

Kaiti scoffed, leaned back and crossed her arms over her chest. The way she managed to make the pissed off, naked, and soaking wet look work for her was impressive.

"I take that as you'll think about it?" I pressed gently. Part of me didn't want to push Kaiti into such a dinner. Her blood pressure was already too high, and I didn't want to do anything to cause her to feel any worse than she already did. "I just miss her, Kaiti, so I said yes. But if you don't or think it's too soon, let me know, and I'll tell her we can't make it this time."

Kaiti's shoulders dropped and her eyes filled with tears. "I *do* miss her. Not that we ever caught up a lot during the semester, but she'd always call or text."

I nodded in understanding and waited for her to continue.

But she didn't. Instead, she laid her head back and was silent, lost to thought.

I got to my feet, walked over to the bathtub, leaned down and kissed her lips. "I've got a bit of work to do for tomorrow. Are you okay if I go get on top of it now?"

"Please do." She smiled at me. "I'll just stay here a while, I think."

"No problem, beautiful," I said chuckling. as I ducked out of the room, leaving her to think. Kaiti often needed time to mull over her choices, and luckily, we had a few days to spare before it became an issue.

Without too much hassle I finished all my work, then we went to bed. I spooned into Kaiti's gorgeous, exhausted body and sighed as our heat mingled, and my body got undeniably hard. "Ignore any poking," I whispered into her ear. "There's no pressure. I have no control over him."

She laughed and took my hand that was resting on her waist and tugged my arm down so that my palm lay flat against her belly.

"It's not that I don't want to see Chastity. I do," she whispered suddenly. "I love our daughter, but I'm so worried about the new baby, and so angry at her and Axel still. I just..." she sighed, clearly conflicted.

I knew how angry she felt, and how worried about her pregnancy she was. So, I said the only thing I could think of. "Shhh..." I whispered, kissing her hair and pulling her in tighter. "Everything will be okay, sweetheart. It'll work out for us all. We just have to have faith. Try to get some sleep, beautiful."

I stayed awake for hours after she dozed off, just holding her and thinking about the future. I'd been so lonely for so many years and I knew she had been too. I'd let my pride and stupidity get in the way of our happiness twenty years ago. And I wouldn't let it happen again.

CHAPTER 3

Kaiti / Katherine

I stared at myself in the mirror, barely recognizing the ghost that stared back at me. "I cannot believe I agreed to this, Patrick."

My handsome man walked up behind me, flashing me a grin in the mirror. "You're doing the right thing, beautiful. We have to break the ice at some point, so why not tonight?"

"Why?" I repeated in frustration. "Because I feel fat, ugly and old! That's why."

He laughed at me, a sparkle in his dark eyes.

I turned around and whacked him on the arm in mock indignation.

"Sweetheart! You're fucking *hot*! I'd honestly bend you over right now and fuck you where you're standing if you'd let me."

I turned back to the mirror, a hot flush rising into my pale cheeks. "You'd ruin my makeup," I said, swallowing the lump in my throat. I had already spent an hour doing my cosmetics, and my blasted hair still wasn't sitting right for me.

Patrick stepped up behind me again and slid his hand around my waist. "You're beautiful as you are," he soothed. "And we're going to be late if we don't make a move, so let's go."

I let out an exhausted sigh, grabbing some candy from the nightstand to help with my blood sugar, and followed Patrick out the door. I was wearing a new, loose-fitting black maxi dress that I'd bought from a maternity store online. It fit well and since I wasn't showing yet, I'd added a large gold belt to match my necklace and earrings. I liked how I looked in my outfit, I just wasn't feeling it, which didn't bode well for how I'd feel walking into dinner with Axel and my daughter.

It only took fifteen minutes to drive to the location. We easily found a parking spot, then walked along the street toward the restaurant I'd never been to before.

"Here it is," Patrick said, opening the door wide for me.

I inhaled sharply as I walked inside. There were barely ten tables in the whole place, each adorned with pure white linen tablecloths and lit by candlelight. "Patrick! We can't afford this place."

He grinned at me and reached for my hand, holding me close. "Don't even think about the money. This is an important night for us all."

I wanted to growl at him for bringing me somewhere I'd feel so out of place and uncomfortable, but then I saw Chastity sitting with Axel on the other side of the room. She was glowing with good health, her skin practically sparkled. My heart tugged with love for my daughter, but there was a deep wave of sadness beneath that emotion as well.

"I see our party. Thank you." Patrick said and tugged me past the stuck-up Matre'd and toward our table.

I smiled at my daughter, but she didn't get up to hug me, so I didn't rush to her either. I sat down next to her, and Patrick sat closer to Axel, which worked for me.

Axel shook Patrick's hand, then turned to me. "Congratulations, Katherine. How are you feeling?" he asked.

Did he really want to know? I brushed my hair back behind my ear and sighed. "Well, nervous to be honest. We have our twelve-week sonogram this week, and more blood tests."

"Why are you nervous, Mom?" Chastity asked, frowning as though she were confused—and she probably was.

I glanced down at my hands in my lap before answering. Chastity was twenty-two, and she wouldn't have considered all the ramifications that came with being pregnant at my age. I coughed to clear my throat, then met Chastity's gaze once more. "The doctors keep referring to my age like my pregnancy is some sort of disease, and I'll feel a lot better once the amniocentesis is done. Did you need to have one of those?" It was doubtful given her age and health, but I thought I'd ask anyway.

"Oh, ah…" Chastity stammered. She didn't even look like she knew what the word meant, let alone what the risks were. The test came with a point five percent chance of miscarrying, which to me was far too high.

"No, I don't think you did," Axel said, cutting in. "You just had the blood test, right?"

Chastity nodded. "Yes, we got the IPSI done."

"Oh?" I asked, surprised they'd wanted even that test, considering how young and healthy Chastity was. "And how did it go?"

Chastity beamed. "It went really well. The baby's healthy, there're no anomalies to speak of, and we got to find out the sex!"

"Oh, we don't want to know. Please don't tell us," I gasped out. I was way too superstitious for that. What if something happened later in the pregnancy and she grew attached? This was going terribly and I felt overwhelmed. I grabbed for Patrick's hand above the table for support.

"Um, okay," Chastity said, her expression now crestfallen. She glanced over at Axel as though he'd have an answer for her.

I couldn't breathe properly.

Axel turned to us. "Are you two finding out what you're having, or would you rather not and leave it as a surprise?"

We didn't have much of a choice. With all the tests and weekly ultrasounds they'd planned for me, I'd know soon enough. "Oh, we'll find out," I said finally, then felt stupid for my response and tried to explain my choice. "But we won't tell anyone. I think that should be kept private until the day the baby arrives, and then we'll announce it."

Chastity stared at me like I'd lost my mind. I had no idea what to say next.

This is awkward and uncomfortable, and I hate it!

Patrick gestured to Axel, clearing his throat. "Shall we order some wine?"

"Definitely." Axel lifted his hand to get the waiter's attention. One hurried over and took their order.

Meanwhile, Chastity and I ordered sparkling water, and I was just hoping I'd be able to keep it down.

Chastity picked up a menu, frowned at the page then said, "Axel…" in a warning tone.

"Just order anything you'd like," he cut her off with a smile.

"But…"

Axel reached for Chastity's hand and kissed her fingers in a way that had me reaching for my menu so I couldn't see him.

There were no prices on any of the pages. *Great.* What my mother had always said to me came back to mind. *"If you need to ask the price, you can't afford it."*

Chastity leaned in. "I think I'll go with the steak. Can you recommend which one would be the best?" she asked Axel.

"Absolutely," he said.

I didn't like this at all and decided to question Axel since he'd chosen the restaurant, obviously on purpose to put us at a disadvantage or flex, I wasn't sure. "How are we supposed to know what this is going to cost us if there are no prices?"

"Dinners on me," Axel said smoothly. "I owe Pat dinner from his fortieth, and I thought we could double up with the joint celebration of our babies."

I clenched my jaw together, hating the way Axel had just assumed he would pay for everyone. That wasn't how we did things in my family. We paid our way.

The waiter came by, and we ordered, though I had to request several changes to the meal I selected, since I couldn't keep much down and knew what my triggers were.

Chastity suddenly turned to her boyfriend, who was only a year younger than I was. "Axel, how's the new management team going? I didn't get to ask you before we came in. Well, I hope?"

"Management team?" Patrick repeated as though that was news to him.

Axel shifted on his chair, seeming uncomfortable.

What's going on now? I wondered.

"Well, I was going to ask you about it, actually, Pat. On our run tomorrow."

They're running together again? Since when? I glared at Patrick, but he failed to notice.

He was too busy asking the next question. "Ask what?"

"Well," Axel began, and glanced over at Chastity. "Well, it was pointed out to me by a few people who shall remain nameless that I'm a bit of a workaholic."

Patrick chuckled and picked up his glass of red wine. "Can't argue with that," he said.

"So, Cheryl at my office has been working on hiring a group of managers to take over some of my tasks. The idea is that it will ideally leave free me to pursue new accounts and perform the executive tasks that I prefer."

Patrick's jaw practically hit the ground. "Seriously?" Patrick asked. "You're actually hiring managers to take on some of your responsibilities?"

"He's delegating," Chastity said with a wide grin.

"I know," her father answered. "I'm just genuinely surprised."

Axel reached over and grabbed Chastity's hand. "I want to slow down for Chastity and the baby. I want to be able to be there for her whenever she needs me."

I swallowed hard, then reached for my glass of water. My stomach was churning more and more with every minute that passed.

"And how many managers are we talking about?" Patrick asked, his tone very business-like as he nodded.

"I've hired three so far. They're all graduates from the same year."

Was he bragging right now? Or was there an undertone I wasn't quite understanding? I made a mental note to ask Patrick later.

"Oh, that's right," Chastity said, joining in the conversation. "You mentioned that Taylor wanted you to interview some of her classmates!"

"Yes," Axel said, grinning back. "And it's working out fantastically. They're all specialized and work efficiently together."

"So, what did you want to talk to me about, then?" Patrick asked.

"I haven't actually mentioned it to anyone just yet, but I was wondering if you would consider coming to work with me?"

I narrowed my eyes at Axel, my heart filling with suspicion. He didn't seriously think that was a good idea, did he?

"In what capacity?" Patrick asked, his tone carefully neutral. "Because we always said we wouldn't work together. It can get messy."

Chastity piped in again. "You and Dad have wanted to work together before?"

Axel nodded. "Yeah, we always said it wouldn't work out. But since we're sort of family now, I just thought I'd ask again."

I inhaled sharply. *Family?* Since when did getting my daughter pregnant and making her drop out of her grad school placement qualify him as our family?

"What's wrong?" Axel asked, his brow creasing.

Patrick shook himself. "In what capacity?" he enquired.

"As my second-in-command," Axel replied. "You'd oversee all the new managers I've hired. They're in their mid-twenties and could use your experience. You'd coach them and keep them from doing anything stupid, more or less."

"Tell me about them," Pat requested.

And Axel did.

There were two women and a man, and they were all stupidly qualified. But all I could think about was that Pat's earlier statement rang true. The notion of how messy things in our life would become if we allowed this to actually happen threatened to drown me alive at the damn table.

Patrick was smart. extremely intelligent, and he could definitely use a new challenge in regard to his job. *But to work for Axel?* I shuddered internally. The billionaire playboy who'd been fucking our daughter behind our backs. How would Patrick ever trust him again?

"I'll come by tomorrow and meet them, if that works for you," Patrick said.

I was shocked to hear him even considering it.

"There's no pressure, of course. You don't have to say yes," Axel told him. "But I need a vice president, and you'd be a perfect fit. But if you don't think you can work with me—"

"You mean *for* you, right?" I interrupted, correcting his grammar. I'd had about enough of the billionaire's flippant holier-than-thou attitude. We didn't need rescuing! Patrick could surely find a better job if he wanted to that didn't involve the man screwing our eldest child.

Axel shifted his gaze over to me. "Sorry?"

I leaned back in my chair and stared straight at him. "You keep saying you want Patrick to work with you, but what you mean is that you want him to work *under* you."

Axel frowned at me, perplexed by my affront. "I'm offering my best friend a job that he would be brilliant at and that pays twice as well as his current position."

He'd be brilliant at any job he set his mind to, I thought. *But that doesn't mean he has to work for you.*

Chastity stared up at her boyfriend and gushed. "That's so thoughtful of you, Axel. Thank you."

Oh, yes. *So thoughtful.* Where was his thoughtfulness when he was lying to Patrick about sleeping with our daughter?

"I should have done it years ago," Axel said, finally looking like he was a little embarrassed.

My gut was churning and the mild headache I'd started the night with had turned into a throbbing and relentless pain inside my skull. "So, why didn't you?" I shot out. "Or, maybe the question is, why are you offering now? For Chastity's benefit? Because it's not for us. Is this some fickle attempt to smooth things over?"

"Kaiti..." Patrick whispered, rolling his eyes at me like I was the one who should be embarrassed.

Well, I wasn't! I just glared back at him.

Axel glanced back at Patrick. "Look, I didn't mean to upset anyone. Maybe we can talk about this another time, Patrick?"

"Yeah. Good idea," my partner agreed.

I bit the inside of my cheek to stop myself from spitting back at them again, but then I caught Chastity's eye, and she looked damn near almost as angry as me.

CHAPTER 4

Kaiti / Katherine

Chastity glared at me. "What's your problem, Mom?"

Axel grabbed her arm as though he could stop her. "Um, Chastity, maybe we should leave it?"

Oh, no. If anyone should be leaving, it should be us, seeing this going downhill real fast.

"No. I want to know," she told him, then turned her attention to me again. "Well?" She raised a single eyebrow and pursed her lips.

Bitch face. Who the hell did she think she was speaking to? "Well, what?" I barked back, glaring at my daughter.

"What's your problem tonight?" Chastity demanded, leaning forward in her chair. "You know there's no paid maternity leave in America, right? So, why wouldn't you encourage Dad to get a better job? A higher paying job?"

This was about money, is it?

Since when did Chastity care so much about money? That wasn't how we'd raised her. Not at all.

Oh, that's right... she was dating a *billionaire* now. *Everything* was about money. "You don't need to concern yourself with our finances, Chastity," I snapped. She never had before. Why should she be worried about us now? "We're perfectly fine, thank you. A lot more comfortable than we were when we had you, that's for sure."

"Good," Chastity said. "Then you won't guilt *this* baby into thinking it's his or her fault that you don't get to do anything!"

Excuse me? I felt my blood beginning to reach boiling point.

Axel tried to stop her once more. "Sweetheart..."

I opened my mouth to tell her exactly what I thought about that ridiculous statement, but then two servers turned up with our dinners, serving all four of us at once.

My chest was heaving, and I was struggling to catch my breath. My head was killing me, and I could practically feel my blood pressure shooting up and through the roof. *This is bad for the baby.*

"Enjoy your meals," the waiters said and left.

As soon as they were gone, I leaned over my vegetarian risotto concoction and hissed. "How dare you?"

Chastity's hand tightened into a fist on the table. "How dare I what?" she hissed back.

"How dare you think you can tell us what to do! You're the one who's repeating all the same mistakes we did, and you think you know better? Well, you don't. You barely know this man, and you're too young to have any baby, let alone *his*. There. I said it." I threw myself back in my chair and crossed my arms over my chest.

Meanwhile, Chastity's face was flushing redder and redder.

I wished I could whisper to Pat. *"What the fuck do we do?"* But it was too late now. I knew the men were looking at us, but I didn't dare drag my gaze from Chastity's tomato-colored face.

Then Axel tried to step in. "Sweetheart..."

Chastity pushed herself to her feet and glared down at me. "So, you think I'm too young to have this baby? Well, I'm older than you were with me! *And* in a thousand times better financial position, so you're wrong, Mom. Totally wrong!"

"You should be going to chiropractic school, Chastity and chasing your dream. Not letting one mistake ruin your future!"

"Ah—" Axel started to interject.

Chastity exploded. "This isn't a mistake!" she screamed into the quiet restaurant. "You're the one making mistakes, getting pregnant at forty-three! But I at least supported you when I saw you needed it. You couldn't even do that!"

I stood up, not allowing Chastity to speak down to me. She had no idea what this meant to me. *To us.* "This baby is our second chance to be together—to be a real family."

Chastity's gasp was loud and cut through me like a knife.

"You and me, Mom—we're done. Enjoy your baby, because you're never going to get to see this one. She's just a mistake, anyway." Chastity cupped her belly, framing her swelling stomach with her hands protectively. "Axel, let's go."

She? Had Chastity just said she? Was she having a little girl? The pain in my head became crippling and I was beginning to get too dizzy to stand, so I sat back down in my chair.

Chastity grabbed all her stuff and twisted around to stomp toward the door like she used to when she was a little girl.

Axel, in his ten-thousand-dollar suit, followed behind her. He spoke to the maître'd in apologetic tones, then stepped outside with Chastity.

I slumped into my chair, groaning at the wave of pain consuming me.

"Kaiti," Patrick said, sliding his hand onto my thigh. "That wasn't smart."

I closed my eyes against the pain and the sense of sorrow that swept up from under me. "I know."

"This was the wrong choice. Dinner," Patrick said, his tone regretful. "You aren't well enough, and there are too many relationship dynamics to try to fix this in one meal." He sighed heavily.

I forced myself to look up. "I…" My throat was thick with emotion and my eyes were beginning to water.

"It's all right," he said, leaning forward to kiss my lips. "I'm going to speak to Chastity. You need to eat something, so you don't faint on the way back to the car. All right?"

I nodded. "Okay." My fork seemed too far away, but I managed to pick it up and use it to scoop up the pumpkin that was just sitting there. The meal itself was presented beautifully, was colorful, and smelled absolutely divine. But my stomach churned and recoiled at the idea of eating anything. It made me feel sick.

"I'll be right back, okay?" Patrick said, squeezing my hand. "Eat, please." He got up and walked to the front door and stepped outside. He was going to talk to them.

Probably to apologize for my behavior, I thought miserably. I sat up straighter, anger filling my aching gut to replace the self-pity and sadness. How did everyone else manage to pretend that everything was okay? Because it sure as fuck wasn't!

CHAPTER 5
Patrick

I wasn't losing my daughter. *Not today, not ever.* No amount of crazy, pregnancy hormones and unpredictable mood swings would take our daughter from us. This was all temporary. We all had a future together, somehow, I felt sure of it. So, swallowing my pride, I walked to the front door of the restaurant.

Axel moved forward from the outside to open it for me.

Once I stepped out into the cool night air, I looked toward my daughter.

Chastity was barely holding herself together and her eyes were filled with tears and her face was still pink with anger.

I couldn't stop myself from pulling her into my arms. She would always be my little girl, no matter what. "I'm so sorry, Chastity."

She broke into sobs then.

I just held her tightly, wishing with all my heart that I could make everything better. When I pulled back, I held onto her upper arms, hoping she wouldn't faint or swoon, or whatever pregnant women were prone to do when they were unfed and overcome by strong emotions. "I have to get back in there before she blows another gasket," I said. "The doctor said her blood pressure's too high already, and we have to try and keep her calm." And that was a drastic understatement. I didn't want to alert Chastity as to how unwell her mom really had been, but I'd woken up with a fist of pain in my gut every day for a week.

Chastity sobbed out a laugh. "Yeah, good luck with that."

Yeah, thanks, kiddo, I thought. I held out my hand to Axel, determined to keep this as civil as possible. "I appreciate the job offer. I'll be over tomorrow around one pm, if that's okay?"

Axel shook my hand and nodded. "I'll clear the schedule. Thank you, Pat."

I nodded, took a deep breath, and headed back into the restaurant. I'd seen Axel speak to the Matre'd earlier, so I was almost certain we wouldn't be paying for the meal, but even so, I'd pay for the dinner if he hadn't already organized something.

Axel had always been generous with money, but I didn't want him to think we were taking advantage of him.

When I got back to the table, I sat down to my steak. Axel and Chastity's dinner sat untouched on the other side of the table. Hundreds of dollars of food wasted. I picked up my knife and fork and forced myself to eat my whole meal, drinking my wine as I went, despite the glances from the other exclusive patrons. The steak was mercifully amazing. Tender, juicy and perfectly seasoned. I allowed myself a small sigh of satisfaction. "How's your risotto?" I asked Kaiti when I'd finished my meal.

She glared up at me. "What did you say to them out there?"

I picked up my wine glass and took another sip of the imported red. "I told Axel that I'd see him at his office on Monday and meet his team. I'll see if we can work together."

I'd found myself occasionally wondering if Axel was the right employer for me. He was smart, strategic, and hard working. If I hadn't known him for a decade as my gym buddy, I would have applied for a job at his company years ago to be honest. He had a nose for business.

Kaiti's eyes widened. "What? I can't believe you did that!"

I put down my glass and turned to look at her. "Axel is a good boss and a motivated, wealthy entrepreneur who built his company from the ground up. I might have some issues about the fact he's in love with our daughter, but... to be honest, I've often considered working for him in the past."

Kaiti softened slightly. "Then why haven't you up until now?"

I nudged her arm toward her dinner.

She automatically put some more of her meal in her mouth.

"Because I didn't want to risk our friendship. But now, what else have we got to lose? Our friendship has changed irrevocably, anyway, so we may as well build it into whatever we want." Not to mention the fact that I'd be getting paid enough money to buy Kaiti and our new baby anything their hearts desired. But I wasn't telling her that just yet.

Kaiti was proud about money, often to her own detriment. There were many times I'd offered extra child support or help with Chastity, and she'd refused, believing she had to do it all on her own; that it was somehow nobler to suffer and trudge on than accept financial help.

She nodded and stared down at her meal, looking deflated.

"You know I only want what's best for you and the baby, don't you?" I asked her, watching her carefully.

She nodded but refused to speak.

I sighed. "I know you feel terrible, and you're still angry at Chastity and Axel, and the *whole* situation. I get it. So, how about we call this night a bust, get you home, and we cuddle and watch a movie in bed?"

She lifted her head and stared at me, her eyes filling with fresh tears. "Yes, please."

"Okay," I said, leaning forward to kiss her softly. "I'm going to pay the bill, if there's anything owed. You eat as much as you can, and then we'll head home."

Kaiti smiled and tucked into her dinner with renewed gusto.

Axel had already paid the bill, of course, but I knew Kaiti would feel better if she thought we were square; so, I sent Axel my thanks via text and took my beautiful woman home.

She cried in my arms until she fell fast asleep, weak and fatigued. Kaiti was spent, both mentally and physically. This second pregnancy was taking a heavy toll on her. It was a whole new experience for the both of us, and not entirely in the best way so far.

My heart ached for her.

CHAPTER 6

Patrick

Taking Monday afternoon off work, I made my way to Axel's building. I arrived half an hour early, just so I could suss things out before anyone knew I was there.

The building itself was one of the tallest in the city, with clean lines and a pleasing aesthetic. The main foyer was impressive, minimalist in style, and always clean with vibrant, live plants artfully decorating the space. It exuded an atmosphere of wealth and prestige without being ostentatious about it. The entire place seemed to say, *'I'm here to do business, not fuck around'*.

I'd been here a few times before but had largely avoided it in the past. Looking back, I'd subconsciously considered this company out of bounds. For some reason, I'd felt Axel's company was too good for the likes of me, and I let my pride and misgivings about our friendship get in the way of a greater future. But I had a partner again, and a new baby to provide for now. And nothing was getting in my way when it came to creating the life we wanted.

Not only that, but I missed Chastity, as well as Axel's friendship. So, I was onboard to do whatever I needed to do to get those relationships back on track; even if it meant working for Axel's company. No doubt, if all went well, it'd go a long way to smoothing things over and bring us all closer together again.

I checked in with the admin in the foyer, then headed up to the top floor, where Axel's personal domain began. As soon as the doors opened, Cheryl spotted me. She was a legend; the dragon who'd been with Axel since his first day on the job. She was the real gatekeeper and without her, I had serious doubts whether Axel would have ever made it this far.

"Patrick," she greeted with her characteristic half smile. "I have you on the schedule for one PM." She waited for my response, like being early was just as impolite as being late.

I tried not to laugh. "Yeah, I was hoping you'd let me check out the new team without them knowing I was here."

Cheryl's smile was fuller this time. She actually looked amused. "I could do that," she said. "Mr. Patterson is out and will be back in about twenty minutes."

I rubbed my hands together. "Excellent. Show me the way, Cheryl."

She actually grinned at me this time, and tilted her head so I would follow her lead. "This way."

I followed her to a large conference room. The door was open, and there was a coffee machine fixed against one wall.

"Cappuccino?" she asked, walking straight into the room and getting to work before I could even answer.

"Yes, please," I responded, though I'd already had enough caffeine for the day.

Cheryl took her time preparing everything so that I could watch the trio at my leisure. All three were in their mid-twenties, dressed in corporate suits, and the normal business armor. However, what made them interesting was the way they spoke to each other.

They started their conversations in English, then swapped to French, then to another language I didn't recognize. All three of them knew what was going on and they hopped from their chairs, to standing, to making notations on the white board, and then they were back to their laptops again. And they didn't stop! The energy in the room was electric and enthusiastic, with lots of competition—but in a good way. The manner in which they worked reminded me of a football team I played on in college... but in a corporate setting. It was amazing to watch.

Axel had really made a great decision in hiring these three.

"Have a seat," Cheryl said finally, indicating a chair for me and placing my cappuccino on the table. "It won't be long."

She left me to sit there and observe them, and although they cast me a smile once or twice, they were too engrossed in their project to really pay me any attention.

At one PM I got up and went in search of Axel's office. I knocked on his door and walked inside to grin broadly at my friend. "Those three are going to take over this company, Axel. You're in trouble."

If he gave them the opportunity, they'd take his company to new heights. They were young and would need guidance, but the potential there was amazing. I could see that even with a blindfold on.

Axel laughed and closed his laptop with a smile. "You've been here less than a minute and you've already worked that out?" he asked.

"I got here half an hour ago, actually, and have just been hanging out with Cheryl and listening in on the three of them. They swap between English, French, and some other language I didn't recognize." Which in itself really impressed me. It meant they could easily expand Axel's business and act as interpreters when necessary. Not to mention being multi-lingual also showed highly developed right brains.

Axel gestured to the seat in front of his desk. "Do you want to sit and chat?"

Sit and have a normal, stressful, bullshit interview? No thank you. "Nah. I was thinking we could go out for lunch and talk there? I'm starving and I know you haven't eaten yet." He never did. Axel stayed lean because he rarely ate during the day, he was just too busy most of the time to breathe.

My friend stood up and walked around the desk, a smirk on his face. "Do you want to take the three vicious babies?" he asked.

I shook my head. "No. I already know I want to work with them." And I'd develop my relationship with them over time. It was Axel's friendship I needed to rebuild right now.

"So, you're in?" Axel asked, his tone matching the excitement I saw in his eyes.

I nodded, nerves twisting my gut. This was a huge step, but it was the right one. I knew it. It was time to expand my horizons beyond my comfort zone. I'd been complacent and bored for far too long; and even worse, for far too little pay.

Axel narrowed his eyes at me. "Don't you want to know the salary? Benefits?"

Why? I already knew they'd be better than what I currently had by a landslide. I laughed. "Axel, I know how generous you are. I know I've always given you hell for your success and your money, and all that shit, but..." I admired the man. I did. I always had. I just had no idea how to tell him that.

"Hey, look. Don't get soft on me. Here." Axel turned around and picked up some paperwork from his desk and handed it to me. "This is only the initial offer."

I took the paperwork and realized it was a contract. He'd already drafted one up? Had he been that confident that I'd want to work here? I had to read it. No point going to lunch if I didn't know what I was accepting, or if we were moving forward. If he was ready, so was I.

Axel moved back around his desk and sat back in his executive chair.

I read the whole thing, shocked at how truly generous Axel was being. *Is this standard?* I wondered. Or was he giving me extra due to Chastity and my relationship? I didn't want that. Taking advantage of him wasn't my deal. "A car?" I asked, glancing up at him. Was he serious? I already had a car, as he knew, but Kaiti could definitely use an upgrade—she certainly deserved one after all these years.

"Yes," Axel said, nodding once.

"Top tier health benefits?" I continued, reading through again.

"Yes. For you and your whole family," he said.

Tightness wrapped around my chest as I read the figure at the bottom of the first page again. "My salary—" *is freaking insane!* It was almost three times what I currently made. This would be life changing for me, Kaiti, and our baby.

"Not enough?" Axel asked suddenly, jumping to the edge of his chair. "We could set some bonuses based on performance?" he offered.

Was he serious? He wanted to offer me more? *No way.* "I need two weeks to tie up some loose ends at my current position, then I can start."

"As easy as that?" he asked, looking shocked.

I nodded. "Yeah, as easy as that. Have you got a pen?" If he thought I was letting him change his mind, he was insane.

Axel pushed a pen across the desk toward me.

I picked it up and signed on the dotted line without thinking twice. "Done."

Axel shook his head. "I can't believe we're finally going to work together!"

Me, neither. "Even though we said we never would." I shook my head and pushed the signed document across the desk back at the man who was officially now my boss.

Axel stood up and walked around the desk, grabbing his jacket. "And now, lunch to celebrate."

"On you," I said with a grin. Not that I couldn't afford it now.

"Of course," he answered with his tell-tale grin.

An hour later we'd drunk a bottle of red wine and eaten a couple of steaks and were sitting in one of our favorite restaurants on a late Monday afternoon.

"Don't you have to get back to work?" I asked Axel.

He took a sip of his water after four glasses of wine. "Don't you?" he countered.

I shrugged. "I took the afternoon off." And it was time to celebrate, anyway. I had a new job, and my best friend and I were on track to getting our friendship back to where it should be.

"Then I will too!" Axel declared, then ordered us another bottle of red. "I still owe you that birthday meal, and since the other night got shot to hell... we can pretend this is your birthday lunch."

I groaned and ran both hands over my face. "Fuck, that was *ridiculous*. Kaiti is so worried about everything at the moment, and it makes her crazy." In fact, I was becoming seriously worried about her mental health. I didn't think depression was meant to hit until after the baby was born, but I needed to talk to her doctor and see what we could do. She was really struggling.

"Can I ask you something?" Axel said.

"Sure," I answered, though I was going to need more fortification for this conversation. I picked up the bottle of red and poured us both another glass. "At this point in time, I don't think we should have any secrets."

"Why now?" Axel asked, as though he didn't know.

Do I really have to spell it out? "Because you got my daughter pregnant, and I saw you two naked in your apartment. I don't think we can get much closer than that, man."

Axel burst out laughing, his eyes shining with mirth. "Okay, but I just wanted to know how you're doing, you know with the pregnancy. Katherine's, I mean. Are you happy about being a dad again?"

"Are you happy about being a dad for the first time ever?" I shot back at him.

A grin spread over Axel's face. "I couldn't be happier. This baby is the best thing that's ever happened to me, except for Chastity of course, and it's not even here yet."

"*She's* not even here yet," I corrected remembering Chastity's slip up over dinner, then sighed. I was still wrapping my head around it. "I'm going to have a granddaughter. I can't really believe it."

Axel huffed out a laugh. "I can't believe my daughter is going to be your granddaughter, man. But, hey... stranger things have happened."

"Name one," I challenged him.

Axel couldn't, but that didn't stop us from having one of the best afternoons I'd had in a very long time.

CHAPTER 7

Kaiti / Katherine

I stared at my doctor, convinced I hadn't heard her correctly. I couldn't have. "Sorry... can you say that again? I don't think I heard you properly."

My doctor sighed and turned away from the computer screen where my blood tests screamed 'unhealthy'.

"You need to be on bed rest, Katherine," she said without preamble. "I'm sorry to say it. I know you love your job, but I am going to write you a letter for the next six months."

I gaped at her. "I... I don't love my job *that* much. But I've been doing it for over fifteen years. And financially..." My job had supported me and had kept Chastity clothed and fed all this time, not that Patrick hadn't helped financially. He always had. But I liked being independent and taking care of myself.

The doctor stared at me. "I'm sorry to give you this news Katherine, but I need to provide you with the best medical advice possible—for you and the health of your baby. Your blood pressure is dangerously high and you're not eating enough. You're also not sleeping, and the baby is in the tenth percentile for height and weight."

I swallowed hard. "And the tenth percentile is bad?" I ventured.

She pressed her lips into a thin line. "Fiftieth is average, tenth is getting very small, and since you're very certain on conception dates, we know that the baby is truly the age that we believe it is."

I blew out a breath, my heart breaking at the thought of my baby suffering because of me. "Okay... so the baby is small because my body is failing?"

"Your body is not failing. Your body is amazing. You conceived this baby naturally, and despite all the stress that's happening in your life, you're both still standing, so to speak. But you *need* to rest. In fact, I'm going to put you on four weeks bed rest from today to start with."

I gasped, then glared at her. "You wouldn't!" A sense of betrayal filled my veins.

She smiled in the face of my anger. "I certainly would. Do you have anyone who can help you at home?"

Did I? I wasn't asking Charity, that was for damn sure.

"What about your daughter?" my doctor asked gently.

I shook my head. "No. She's just graduated college. I saw her last week." *And what a reunion that had been!* The day I'd looked forward to for years and years had been a stiff, stilted night that had left me feeling hollow and alone. Patrick was the only reason I hadn't spent the whole night crying.

The doctor continued. "Surely, she can bring over food and help out—"

"No," I snapped. "She's moved in with her boyfriend." Though that man was definitely not a *boy*. "And she's pregnant, also. She's measuring four weeks ahead of me."

The doctor's eyes widened a little. "Wow... that's special. Being able to share your pregnancy journeys together."

It would have been. It should have been. But... I tried to stay calm and explain to the doctor that our relationship wasn't up to that sort of stress at the moment, but I couldn't speak. Instead, I tried inhaling sharply through my nose, but my eyes began to burn, and my throat closed up.

The doctor moved the tissue box closer. "What's happened, Katherine? This is a safe space. You're welcome to talk to me."

I burst into tears. I couldn't help it. I sobbed and sobbed, letting out so many of the painful feelings from the past few months that had been slowly building up to crash down on me like a tidal wave so heavy I could no longer bear it. Chastity's college graduation had been a bittersweet event for me and Patrick.

We'd worked *so* hard to give her every opportunity that we'd never had. She'd received a great education, then secured a place in chiropractic school. We'd had such high hopes for her future. But just like me, she'd gotten pregnant and now her future was... well... ruined.

My doctor got me a glass of water from the water cooler in the corner of the room.

The crying began to slow down and after I'd blown my nose and mopped up the tears on my face, I sipped on the water she gave me. Strangely, I was still feeling embarrassed, but slightly better having decompressed a little.

"Now, tell me what that was," she said gently.

I sighed heavily. I hadn't told anyone except Patrick about what Chastity and I were going through, but it felt good to have someone else to talk to. "Basically, my daughter and I aren't really speaking. I'm not happy that she fell pregnant before she even graduated college, to a guy she's known for less than six months, and I don't have the energy to even try."

The doctor smiled softly, then pushed over the letters she'd printed out. "It sounds like you need to sort out everything with your daughter at your own pace. Speak to Patrick. See if you can get a little help at home, because I want you in bed as much as physically possible, Katherine. Only getting up to go to the bathroom or shower. Eat in bed. Read in bed. Netflix in bed."

I groaned. "But my students..."

She gave me the strong, resolute 'don't fuck with me' face. "Katherine, your baby's health is literally on the line here. Do I need to call Patrick?"

I reached for the letters I'd need to send in to work. "No. We'll sort something out, I'm sure," I managed stiffly.

Patrick had already offered financial support, and I was pretty sure Mom and Dad would help with meal preparations and cleaning.

"I could probably get you into the hospital for a few weeks if you need some round the clock care," the doctor offered.

"Oh, no, no," I said, picking up my bag and standing. "I'd much rather be at home. I just need to wrap my head around all these changes, that's all." Not to mention the fact I would miss Patrick incredibly if I was in hospital for two weeks. He'd come to visit, but we'd have no privacy.

The doctor smiled. "Your whole life is about to change again, Katherine. Another baby after raising your first to adulthood is a big deal. It's okay not to be all right *all* the time."

I smiled for the first time since arriving. "I know, but this is our second chance. For our relationship, for our whole family." And it was the only thing that kept me sane through the never-ending nausea and fatigue.

"Then focus on that," she said, walking me to the door. "While you're resting, think about that second chance and what it means for the rest of your life."

I smiled again and thanked the doctor for her help. Then I drove home, pretty sure that had been against the rules, but not wanting to screw up multiple people's day because we needed to go back and fetch my car. Once I got home, I emailed work the news, then crawled into bed and slept the day away.

When Patrick got home, he'd brought pizza and garlic bread. I could smell it. The usually delicious aroma made me feel a little yucky, but I needed food, so I'd force it down—for the baby. "Hey, hon!" I called out. "I'm in here."

He walked in looking too handsome for words, carrying plates and pizza boxes. "I thought you might be resting when you didn't answer your phone. Is everything okay?"

I groaned. "Sorry, love, it was on silent because of the doctor's office policy. They don't allow phones. Then I was so tired I just forgot to turn it back on when I got home." I opened the smaller box and tried hard not to breathe as I picked up a slice of my favorite cheese pizza and took a bite.

Patrick was staring at me like he'd never seen me eat before.

"What?" I asked, chewing away.

"Um, nothing. I just... I only got you the small because you haven't been eating lately. I would have gotten you a large like mine if I'd known you were up to eating it. Sorry, sweetheart."

I choked down the pizza, then reached for my bottle of water next to the bed. "The doctor said I've lost too much weight, and I have to eat more." My stomach actually felt a little better having some food in it, so I grabbed the slice up again and took another bite.

Patrick gave me the side eye. "I've been telling you that for *three* months," he said flatly.

I smiled at him, though my chest was tight with the knowledge that I'd have to tell him our news. "Well, it seems that I have to listen now," I answered. "The doctor has told me I can't work anymore, and that I'm on bed rest for a month."

Patrick's mouth dropped open. "Seriously? How bad is it, Kaiti? What aren't you telling me?"

I wiped at the tear that had sneakily leaked out onto my cheek. "It's bad. The baby's too small, like way under average, and my blood pressure's still super high. She... I... I don't think the baby will be born healthy unless I stop *everything* and rest."

Patrick moved the food to the dressing table, kicked off his shoes, then climbed under the covers with me. "You are doing amazing, sweetheart. I don't want you to ever think badly of yourself for any of this, okay? Later pregnancies are hard on the body, you know that. But I believe in you, Kaiti. You can do this, and I'm right here with you—all the way."

"Okay," I managed to say, though my throat felt thick with emotion once more.

Patrick wrapped his arm around my shoulders. "I'm going to rent out my place and move in here as soon as possible, if that's still okay with you? And I'll get you set up with access to all my bank accounts too, okay?"

I stared up at him. "I have savings, Patrick, and the house is mostly paid off."

"We're a couple, right?" Patrick asked. "A committed, in love couple, who are working toward a future together that's going to include the next fifty years or so, right?" he pressed.

I raised an eyebrow at him. "Fifty years?" I gulped. *I'll be ninety by then!*

He shrugged. "I can dream. But my point is, who cares if I pay for a few extra things this year? I might need your help in the future. You never know what's going to happen in life. Just look at us now. We just have to ride the way together."

I nodded slowly. "That's true."

"So, let's truly begin our lives together, okay?" he said. "You don't have to worry about money anymore, no stress. We can eat takeout every night if you want, and we can even get a housekeeper or someone in if you'd like! Whatever makes life easier for you, beautiful."

I stared up at him. "Really?" Was it really possible that he'd want to support me so much? Patrick really was the love of my life. *He always has been.*

Patrick laughed in that easy, happy way that had charmed the pants off me since I first met him. "Of course! I can't carry the pregnancy for you, sweetheart, but I *can* and *will* help you with everything else possible."

I reached for a tissue, blew my nose, then smiled up at my gorgeous man. "How about more pizza?" I asked, feeling a little stronger than I had been.

He grinned at me. "Absolutely." Patrick grabbed the boxes and dragged them back to the bed. And then we spent the rest of the night chatting and eating and sleeping in the bed that would be my whole world for at least the next month solid.

CHAPTER 8
Patrick

The next month flew by at work. I finished up with my old crew, then began working with Axel. I spent my days managing three of the brightest people I'd ever met and trying not to get in Axel's way. He was a rock, and a powerhouse of a man. I'd always admired his work ethic, but working alongside him gave me a new understanding and appreciation of him.

"Are you heading home?" Axel called to me.

I picked up my suit jacket and slid it on. "Yeah." I said, making sure I had everything I needed; laptop, keys, and cell phone. "I've got to pick up dinner on the way."

"And how is Kaiti doing?" Axel asked, leaning back against my desk.

I cringed without meaning to. "She's... okay. She's not liking being chained to a bed all day, but the doctor said the baby's growing, and Kaiti's blood pressure is steadily going down. How that's possible, I have no idea. But..." I shrugged. Getting in a housekeeper had been expensive, but between the extra money from my new job, and moving out of my apartment, we'd more than made up for the extra expenses.

Axel nodded and hummed.

"And how's my daughter doing?" I asked him with a grin.

"She's good," Axel said casually. "She wants to buy a house, so we're looking at one tomorrow."

I gaped at him. "You're buying her a house?"

Axel chuckled. "Of course. The apartment's not really infant friendly, and Chastity wants a pool and a big backyard, so why not? If she's happy, I'm happy. You know what they say, happy wife, happy life!"

I clapped him on the shoulder. "You're a good man, Axel." It was *so* freaking odd to have to flip from employee to father-in-law, almost in the same sentence. But we were making it work. "I'll see you tomorrow," I said with a grin.

"Yeah, cool. Thanks for today, Pat."

I nodded at him and headed out to pick up the Chinese food order Kaiti had already placed. When I got in the car, I called my daughter. "Hey, sweetie."

"Hi, Dad! How are you doing?" Chastity answered in high spirits.

"I'm good, just on my way home and thought I'd give you a call and check up on everything. Are you good? Baby good?"

"Yeah, we're both well, thanks Dad. I'm going a little stir crazy, though."

I could imagine. Chastity always did like to be busy. "Axel said something about you guys looking at a house tomorrow?" I prompted.

"Yeah, we are! The house I like needs some renovations, but it's in a *great* area and I've just got a really good feeling about it. It feels like it could be home, you know?"

"Sounds awesome," I said, a smile on my face. "Can you send me the link so I can check it out too?"

There was a long silence. "Are you going to show Mom?" she asked.

I inhaled sharply, thinking about the best way to answer that, I knew my girls were still at odds and no progress had been made to mend the damage done over that fateful dinner. "I was going to, but if you don't want me to, I won't." My phone *tinged!* with a message.

"I sent the link through," she said.

She didn't say anything about not telling Kaiti, so I moved on. "Okay, hon. Well, I've got go get some takeout then get it home to Mom."

"How's she doing?" Chastity asked tentatively.

I rolled my eyes, wishing these two would just get their shit together sooner, rather than later. "She's like you to be honest, going stir crazy at home. She's on bed doctor mandated rest, so there's not much for her to do."

Chastity gasped and it actually sounded like she cared. "Is the baby okay?" she asked, her voice wobbling ever so slightly.

"Yeah, they're both okay for the moment. We just have to be careful with her. Maybe you could message her and check in on her once in a while, huh? She'd really like that, kiddo."

"Okay, Dad. Goodnight."

"Night, sweetie." I hung up then heaved a massive sigh. I hated the fact Kaiti and Chastity weren't getting along. I really did. In the past, I might have enjoyed it—being the favorite for a hot minute—but now that Kaiti and I were back together, it just wasn't good at all. Kaiti was miserable, and things with Chastity were awkward too.

I got home to a clean house and a cranky Kaiti. She was sitting up in bed with the covers up to her waist, a pile of books next to her.

"Dinner delivery!" I called, grabbing some bowls and cutlery to bring with me.

"Grab the tray too please, hon!" she called. "Nancy cleaned *every-thing* today! When I was taking a shower, she even stripped the bed and remade it fresh."

I grinned at her tone as I set everything up on the clean bed and opened the plastic containers. I was putting on a bit of weight eating like this all the time, but I figured I had the rest of my life to work out at the gym. The most important thing was that Kaiti was gaining weight again. Her cheeks had filled out and her breasts were plump and full. And I knew if I started showing any signs of worrying about my weight, her self conscious streak would rear its ugly head.

"Why does that sound like a bad thing?" I asked, a smile quirking my lips.

"She didn't even ask me!" Kaiti exploded. "I don't even like these covers."

I glanced down at the pretty blankets and back up at Kaiti again. "I think you're over-reacting, sweetheart. The bed looks lovely."

Kaiti glared at me and snatched up the spring rolls. "Maybe I am, but I feel like I'm going crazy here!"

"You're doing amazing, beautiful, even the doctor said so! And your bed rest ends technically tomorrow, so I thought you'd be celebrating by now?"

Kaiti grumbled about work and being bored and something else I didn't quite catch.

So, having learned not to allow her mood swings to affect me negatively, I just served myself, grabbed the remote and jumped into bed with her. "Well, I'm happy to be home." I laid a kiss on her luscious lips and began eating. "I'm starving." I'd eaten lunch around twelve but had nothing else since.

"Ah… do you think we could maybe try something tonight?" Kaiti asked cautiously.

"Like what?" I answered as I continued to eat, thinking she was referring to something to do with a new Netflix series. "We can do anything you want, beautiful."

"Could we make love, maybe?" she said hopefully.

I blinked at her then forced myself to swallow the giant spoonful of fried rice in my mouth before speaking, so that I didn't choke and cough up food all over the freshly made bed. "Um, I'd fucking love to. But are we allowed to; I mean… given your state?"

Kaiti gave me a look that made me feel about fifteen years old again.

"What?" I asked defensively. "I'm allowed to ask! I'm just trying to be safe. I don't want to hurt you."

Kaiti sighed. "I spoke to the doctor today. *Again.* And she said that as long as we aren't swinging from the chandeliers or anything, it should be fine. In fact, she suggested that the feel-good hormones would probably benefit my mood."

You can say that again! I put my food aside and began tugging at my tie. "Now?" I asked. "Because I'm *so* ready."

Kaiti laughed aloud.

It made my heart sing. It had been too long since I'd heard her laugh like that.

"No," she said pushing at my chest playfully. "Eat first. But I was just thinking, rather than having a lazy Netflix night, we could have a... well, you know!"

"A sex night?" I asked, kissing her lips and tasting the sweet honey and soy noodles she'd just been eating. "Hell, yes! I've missed being inside you." I picked up my food again to finish my meal.

Kaiti blushed prettily as she stared down at her own food, poking it around with her fork.

I ate quickly, then jumped up, ready for action.

She stared up at me with wide, vulnerable eyes. "Where are you going?"

"To take a shower." I grinned. "I need to wash the day off of me so that I can come and ravish you." I winked at her as her lips twisted into a smile, then marched into the ensuite for my shower. I'd gone to the gym before work and had a quick shower there, but that didn't mean I was clean. Quite the opposite.

I scrubbed myself thoroughly, in between my toes and under my fingernails. It had been months since I'd been able to do more than spoon Kaiti tenderly in the middle of the night, and I'd been wishing I could make love to her like I used to. Once I was sparkling clean and feeling refreshed, I turned the water off and jumped out of the shower, before reminding myself to slow the fuck down.

I dried myself and tried not to run out of the bathroom, half afraid she had changed her mind in the ten minutes I'd been gone. "Steady," I told myself. "Steady." I didn't want to spook her if she was feeling fragile. I really wanted her, so would take it slow. I walked back into the bedroom still naked, to find that Kaiti had moved most of the food onto the dresser, pulled down the bed covers, and was now lying on her back in her underwear and nothing else.

"Oh, wow," I whispered, my gaze sliding over her body. "You're even more beautiful than I remember."

She giggled and rolled onto her side, cradling her stomach. "And look, my belly's getting bigger!"

It was, as were her gorgeous, milky breasts. My cock began to throb, growing of its own volition as I stood there. For several breathless moments I stayed exactly where I was, even though I was dying to jump on top of her.

Kaiti was drinking me in, staring at the proof of my undying attraction to her.

I grinned and put my hands on hips. "I think *he* likes your new curves, beautiful."

She looked up at me through her dark lashes, sultry and seductive. "And you, Patrick? Do you like what you see?"

"Oh, I can't wait to get my lips around one of your nipples and suckle on those luscious boobs."

She reached behind her back, and she must have unclipped her bra, because her full breasts came tumbling out and the bra was cast off the bed.

I licked my lips. "Was that an invitation?"

She nodded, teasing her lower lip between her teeth, reminding me of a much younger Katherine.

I kneeled on the bed, falling down beside her to pull my woman into my body and kiss her.

Her hands pressed against my chest, and she was warm and soft in my arms. Her tongue sought mine, and I kissed her hard in return, my hand stroking down her naked back and loving the feel of her soft skin beneath my fingers. It had been far too long.

When we broke the kiss to breathe, I chuckled as I laid my forehead against hers. "If I'd known this was going to happen, I would have prepared better. I'm afraid I won't last two minutes with you. I've missed you *so* much."

She giggled and lifted her head so that I was looking into her eyes once more. "I've missed you too," she whispered.

I stroked my hand over her growing baby bump, appreciating the feel of her flesh changing due to our child—my child. "Are you sure?" I asked once more.

She nodded and reached her hand down between us, wrapping her warm fingers around my cock. "Absolutely," she breathed against my lips.

CHAPTER 9
Kaiti / Katherine

What Patrick didn't realize was that I had missed him just as much as he'd clearly been missing me. And despite the sickness and the lethargy, my body had been *craving* him for weeks. It'd been utterly infuriating and going without him added to my dour moods.

Then, this morning I'd woken up from the hottest, sexiest dream, and called my physician immediately to find out what I could do about the fact that my hormones were going crazy on me. The doctor had laughed and explained that I didn't have any reason not to have sex with Patrick. My cervix was good, the baby was doing well, and as long as I didn't get my heart rate up unreasonably high, we'd be just fine.

Thankfully, knowing Patrick, that wasn't going to be a problem for us. With our dynamic, he'd always been the one carrying the heavy exertion part of our fucking.

Without hesitation I grabbed his erection, reveling in the fact he was already hard and hot and ready for me. Then I rolled over and said something I'd never said before in my whole life, even when we were happily together two decades ago. "Would you come up here and fuck my face?" I asked.

If I'd had a camera, I would have taken a photo of Patrick's face, just so I could look at it anytime I liked. His expression was a turbulent combination of shock and awe, which soon transformed into downright delight and lust.

He jumped up onto his knees, threw a leg over my head, then fed his cock straight into my mouth.

I moaned at the taste of him on my tongue once more. The delicious heat of his skin against my lips.

Then he began to rock his hips, truly fucking my face, just like I'd asked.

My pussy clenched in envy. I tried not to giggle at my body's jealous reaction, and instead focused on sucking Patrick's gorgeous cock. I hadn't wanted to get up off the bed or drop down on my knees because of my blood pressure. So, this was fucking perfect. I could lie down, relax, and still pleasure my beautiful man.

He pulled back suddenly, groaning as he gripped his shaft hard. "Oh, God, you've got to stop or I'm going to come right down your throat before we even begin."

I did giggle this time when he moved back down the bed. "I'll take that as a compliment," I said, pleased with myself.

"You should," he said, moving to kneel beside the bed before pushing my legs apart.

I groaned loudly when his tongue swiped against my clit, then gasped as my pussy tightened in response. "Oh, Patrick. That feels... *amazing*." I closed my eyes and threw my head back against the pillow, luxuriating in the plethora of sensations assaulting me as Patrick ate my pussy like a starving man.

He flicked my clit from side to side, then licked at my core. Every touch of his tongue or lips pushed me higher and faster toward orgasm. I was so damn sensitive it was mind blowing. And when he finally brought his fingers up and slid them inside me, I shattered.

I cried out as I came all over his hand. My belly convulsed and tightened, and I grabbed onto the swell of my tummy as I shook with the raw intensity of it.

Patrick kissed my thighs and belly, then slid his fingers out so he could crawl up and hold me as I shook in his arms.

"Whoa," I gasped. "That was amazing," I moaned after, still enjoying the aftershocks as I came down.

Patrick grinned as he kissed the tip of my nose. "And I thought I'd be the one to come first."

I shook my head, hardly able to keep my eyes open as a wave of fatigue crashed over me. "No way."

"Here, beautiful. Put your head down and sleep," he said, trying to draw me onto his chest.

I pushed against him. "No! I want you to fuck me."

"How?" he asked. "I assume from behind would be the most comfortable?"

I wanted him on top of me, but he was right. Squashing my belly would freak both of us out. I rolled over, resting on my elbows and pushed my ass up at him. "How's this?" I grinned.

He lifted my upper leg slightly, adjusting his position and slid down so that he could line up our bodies. "That is perfect," he whispered, then grabbed his cock and set it to my entrance.

I pushed back desperately, needing more, my wet pussy allowing him to slide straight into me. I gasped out as he forged inside me, filling me up and making me moan. A tidal wave of pleasure flooded me, causing me to squeeze my eyes shut and my pussy to contract around him.

Patrick held very still as he grabbed my hip. "Are you okay?" he asked.

I nodded, then realized he might not be able to see me from behind. "Yes!" I assured him. "Please, don't stop."

Taking my word for it, he pulled back, then slid into me again.

Desire swept through me, and I gasped, grabbing his hand at my hip. I interlinked our fingers, feeling our connection lock and click into place. I loved this man with every fiber of my entire being, and this physical expression of our love only served to amplify my feelings for him.

He began to move faster, giving into his own pleasure, pumping in and out of me like a well-oiled, sexy machine.

I shuddered and moaned in ecstasy, my starving body reveling in every thrust of his perfect cock within me. Then, before I knew what was happening, I was cresting once more.

Patrick thrust into me hard and deep, then hot streams of his cum filled me up, making my body clench and tighten.

My body contracted and bucked against him as I milked his cock, screaming out again as I came with him still inside me.

Soon after, we collapsed onto the mattress, the air filled with the scent of our sex and the sound of our breathy moans and desperate gasps of satisfaction. We had a short shower when we were able to move once more, then cuddled up in bed.

I didn't want to go to sleep or lose what I was feeling right now. I was so happy and content and well. I'd missed it *and* him so damn much that it pricked my eyes with unshed tears. "Thank you," I whispered up at Patrick, kissing his cheek.

He turned toward me. "For what?" he asked, his brow furrowing.

"For everything," I said. "You've been amazing. Bringing home food every night, renting out your house, getting a housekeeper, and paying for everything."

He smiled. "My job's the easy one, sweetheart. You're the one growing us a second chance baby. You're the amazing one."

I didn't think so. Most days I felt like a failure, at least once a day. But at this moment, he was right. I felt amazing, thanks to him.

"Listen," he said as he cleared his throat. "I don't in any way want to kill the mood, but I know that you like to hear about Chastity news as soon as I know it, so... do you want the day's report? Or do you want to wait until tomorrow?"

I sat up and turned to face him. "You have something to report?"

He nodded, slid out of bed, and walked to the living room. "I'm just grabbing my cell. I'll be back in a second."

I pulled up the blankets, my heart banging harder in my chest. "Calm down. Calm down," I told myself, taking some steadying breaths. The last thing I wanted to do was get worked up for nothing; especially after such an incredibly hot and satisfying session with Patrick.

Patrick walked back into the room with his cell, then slid into bed with me once more. "I spoke to Axel as I was leaving work today and he mentioned that he and Chastity were looking at houses this week. So, I called our daughter and asked her about it."

My chest was tight, but I wanted to know. "A house? Already? What did she say?" I asked anxiously.

"She confirmed that they were looking at a house. She's interested in one that has a big backyard. She said it needs some renovations, but she loves it and really wants something fit to be a family home for the baby."

I inhaled a breath, then blew it out slowly. "Okay, well that sounds like a good idea. Can you show me?"

"I asked her to send me the link of the place they're checking out. I haven't actually looked at it yet. I wanted to show you first." He handed me the phone, then put his thumb on the pad to unlock it. "It's in a text, I think. Let's look at it."

I nodded, grateful he'd waited to check it out with me, but unable to speak. I clicked on the real estate link, and almost instantly gagged at the price. "Two million dollars! Jesus, Patrick. That's insane."

"And it needs work, according to them both so let's have a look at it."

I flicked through the pictures, looking at them through jaded eyes. But even with the salted lens, I could still see why Chastity liked the place. "She picked this one on her own, didn't she?" I could see the tell-tale signs of her taste written all over it.

Patrick nodded. "Yeah, Axel's just trying to make her happy. This is *all* Chasity."

"It has a lot of potential," I managed to say. "It's dated but... it's on a great street, with a huge block... and it's not like they won't have the money to renovate it." And they'd need to spend a whole lot more than two million to bring it up to a standard to live in, but the features were definitely beautiful. With a sigh I pushed the cell phone away and shuffled down into the bed. I was hungry again, amazingly. "I think I want some ice cream," I declared. "Do you want some too?"

Patrick grabbed my arm before I could rise. "You know the rules. You stay, I go."

I rolled my eyes at him. "My bed rest ends tomorrow, officially in like three hours. I can get up."

He mock growled at me.

I had to laugh. "Okay, *all right!* Thank you, honey!"

Patrick disappeared into the kitchen and brought back two bowls of ice cream full to the brim with chocolate and peanuts.

"Oh, yum. Thank you," I said, tucking in with my renewed appetite.

We ate in peace for time before Patrick struck up a conversation. "I hope you're not jealous of what Axel can buy for Chastity, sweetheart. You don't need to be. We might not be able to buy a house like that exactly, but with my new salary, and our two places sold? We could upgrade *very* substantially."

I looked up at him, not even sure how to reply to that.

"Or we could knock this place down and build something newer and bigger? If you don't want to change location?"

I shook my head adamantly. "Oh, no, I couldn't knock this place down." This little house had been my only home for twenty years now. It was Chastity's house. Her growth marks were still on the walls, her bedroom had only ever been her bedroom. "Oh, wow." I sighed. "I hadn't even thought about where the baby would need to sleep. It needs to go into Chastity's room, wouldn't it? So that means cleaning out her room."

"We could add an extension on?" Patrick said. "Another level, maybe? We don't have to get rid of Chastity's room."

I bit my lip, feeling my heart ache with sadness. "No, let's not. You're right. Can we talk about it another day?"

"Of course, we can," Patrick said. "But I want you to know that everything is on the table, Kaiti. New house, new baby, new life. Everything. I want you to be happy and have everything you didn't have the chance to enjoy last time."

I smiled and reached out to cup his face. "I just want you, Patrick. Forever."

"You've got me," he whispered, kissing my lips and holding me tight.

It was a lot to process when I thought about it. My daughter was buying her first house, and she hadn't even bothered to show me or tell me about it herself. On a night where I should feel nothing but happy, there was a small part of me that was still broken. *And I have no idea how to fix it...*

CHAPTER 10

Kaiti / Katherine

I'd made it to six months pregnant and couldn't believe I was still standing! In fact, I was moving around the house, cleaning, and cooking. My blood pressure was manageable, and I'd even found myself looking at real estate pages just to see what was out there. I knew it was unrealistic to think we could stay in this house forever. Patrick and I barely fit, let alone a new baby that would be spoiled in a way that Chastity never was.

That had led to Patrick applying for a new loan and the next thing I knew; we were well on our way to finding the perfect house for our new family. I still couldn't believe it. All those dreams I'd had when I was twenty years old and totally in love with Patrick the first time... they were all coming true this time. A part of me was frightened that at some point, I might wake up to find that all of this—this love, our baby, Chastity and Axel, everything—was all a fever dream. And as much as the billionaire couple were still a thorn in my emotional soul, I wouldn't unwish any of it; not if it meant even the slightest chance I'd lose Patrick.

As it turned out, I wouldn't be going back to work for at least a year after I gave birth, if not longer. And we had money now like I never had

53

before. My new, deluxe and modern stroller cost more than my first car had! It boggled my mind and I pinched myself regularly.

Things with Chastity were still strained, unfortunately. I messaged her every few days just to keep in contact, but she hadn't called to talk, and I hadn't called her either. I felt like a stranger to my own daughter, and it secretly made me angry that Patrick got to see her and talk to her when I didn't. Axel and Patrick were getting along famously, and although I kind of hated it, I was happy for Patrick.

He was content with his job in a way I'd never seen him before, not even twenty years ago. I begrudgingly had to admit that Patrick working with Axel had been the right move, even if I still felt like it was a recipe for disaster. Our whole family could be pulled apart if those two had a spat. Not that we were doing so well even now, but still. I wasn't a fool. I knew things could get a lot worse than they were now.

My phone rang from the kitchen counter, and I grabbed it, expecting it to be Patrick or my mom. They both checked in on me at least once a day. The screen said, **Baby Girl.** I only had one of those... that I knew of at least. We still hadn't found out what the new baby's gender was.

I picked up quickly and cleared my throat. "Chastity, hello." My voice sounded rusty, but I hadn't spoken in over six hours, since Patrick left for work.

"Hey, Mom. How are you doing?"

"I'm fine," I managed to say, though a longer, more involved answer came to mind.

"That's great. Dad said you finished work up early to rest. How's that going?"

I clenched my teeth together. I knew Patrick and Chastity chatted often enough, but I didn't know how much he'd told her about me. Obviously, the answer was *plenty*! "It's tedious," I said then sighed. No point in pretending I didn't know what was going on with her. I did. "Did you take possession of the new house yet?" I asked, changing the subject from me.

There was silence for a moment. "Yeah, we closed a month ago, and it's finally ready to move in. I was wondering if you wanted to come over and see it?"

Of course, I do! I shouted in my mind as if the answer was blood obvious. I'd been dying to see it. But why was she showing me now? Was it out of guilt? Pity? What had spurred her to call today? Finally, I pushed myself to get over my own crap. None of it changed anything and there were bridges that needed to be mended. Sucking it up, I smiled so that my tone of voice sounded brighter. "I'd really like that. What time suits you?" I asked.

"Any time today, if you want? Axel won't be home until dinnertime. Do you want me to send a car around to pick you up?"

She has a car to send to me? That meant that she also knew I wasn't allowed to drive at the moment.

I swallowed down my pride. "Yes. That would be good, thank you."

"Okay, great. His name is Harry and I'll call him now. He'll probably be around soon."

I hung up after we said our goodbyes and stood in the kitchen for too long. I had to call Patrick. With shaking hands, I pressed the buttons, and luckily, he picked up on the first ring.

"Hey, beautiful. How's your afternoon going?" he asked.

"Did you ask Chastity to call me?" I slapped myself on the forehead. *Shit.* I sounded like a bitch. I didn't mean it to sound like that.

"No. I haven't spoken to her for a few days. Why? What's happened?"

I told Patrick about our brief but cordial conversation where Chastity offered me the proverbial olive branch.

He was silent on the other end of the line.

"What's wrong?" I demanded as the silence dragged on uncomfortably.

"Ah... are you ready to see her yet, sweetheart?"

"What do you mean? Of course, I'm ready to see her! It's been months." I'd never gone so long without seeing my own daughter and it was killing me inside.

Patrick sighed. "I know you miss her, but you're going to have to get your head right, Kaiti. She clearly wants to reconcile, not fight."

I frowned at him even though he wasn't there to see it. "I know that." *I think...*

"I'm not sure you do, but okay."

There was a knock at the door, and I twisted around to grab my bag. "The driver is here, hon. I have to go." I didn't want to argue with him about this. I just had to play it by ear and go into it with good intentions.

"Okay, but just remember that this day might make or break your relationship with our daughter, Kaiti. Do *not* go in there angry or hurt, okay? I believe in you. We can be a family again."

I was a bit agitated by his comments, but I knew he was only trying to help. "Thanks, Patrick. I'll talk to you later." Then I hung up and went to the door. It was finally time to see my daughter and the house Patrick had been talking about for months.

CHAPTER 11
Patrick

*S*hit! *Shit! Shit!* Anxiety bubbled within me as Kaiti hung up the phone. I had to act and fast.

One of the three wonder kids called out to me. "Hey Pat! Can we get your help over here for a minute with something, please? We could really use your insight on this one."

I nodded in her general direction, momentarily distracted—my mind elsewhere. "Yeah, sure, not a problem. Just give me two minutes, okay? I need to call my daughter really quick. It's important, sorry!" Then I walked out of earshot, along the sleek hallway and into my private office and shut the door behind me. I had to try and fix this before everything broke beyond repair; before it was too late. I dialed Chastity's number, tapping my foot in impatience as I waited for her to answer. *Please pick up*, I thought. *For the love of God, please pick up!*

"Hey, Dad!" Chastity said when she finally picked up, sounding happy and bright.

Well, that's a good sign to start with. "Hey, sweetie," I said, pacing back and forth. *May as well get to the point*, I reasoned. I was in the middle of a workday and there was no easy way to bring this up. Not to mention that time was of the essence right now. "Ah... have you invited your mom over for a chat just now?" I asked cautiously.

"Obviously she's already told you, so what's the problem, Dad?"

Her annoyance was apparent, but I didn't have the time to pander to her today, too much was at stake. "Well, I just wanted to warn you in advance that she hasn't been in the best of moods lately. She might bite your head off over the smallest thing, so please, please tread carefully."

Chastity sighed. "So, what? What are you... what are you saying exactly, Dad? That I shouldn't have invited her over in the first place? I thought I was doing the right thing."

No! The fact that Chastity had reached out had made Kaiti's entire month. *So, how did I approach this in a better way?* "No, sweetheart. I'm glad you did. It's definitely the right thing, and I'm grateful, actually. She's been harassing me for months for photos and details of you and your life. She's really missed you. Now, she can finally see for herself and speak to you in person." Maybe that was a bit of an exaggeration, but still, it needed to be said. *Better safe than sorry.*

"If she wanted to see me or our house so badly, why didn't she just ask?" said Chastity with an edge of attitude.

Seriously? For fuck's sake, kiddo. "You know why, Chastity." Now wasn't the time for games.

Chastity sighed again, her voice cracking with emotion unexpectedly. "It's just... she's missed my whole pregnancy, Dad," she managed. "It wasn't meant to be like this. I didn't want it to be."

My heart broke for the both of them. "I know. And you're missing hers, too." Both of my girls were going to regret this time for years to come when all was said and done, I was sure of it. But they still had a chance to mend what was broken and I prayed they both took that chance to heart. They were both stubborn as hell, but they loved each other. There was no doubt. They were two peas in a bloody pod!

There was the faint sound of a doorbell chiming in the background. "I think she's here," Chastity said.

Damn it. Of course, she was. The drive between the two houses was super short, which under any usual circumstance would be great. "Okay. Well, please just be careful, Chastity. You're both the most important people in the world to me, and I don't want either of you hurt or upset." And they had been angry for too long; both blaming each other, with neither one willing to bend or yield. *The apple certainly didn't fall far from the tree, that's for sure.*

"I'll try not to upset her, Dad, I promise. But I'm getting a bit sick of dancing on eggshells around her. I feel like I've been doing it my *whole* life. It's exhausting and even more so, now."

I sighed and ran a frazzled hand through my hair. "Yeah, I understand that completely, sweetheart. And any other time, I'd tell you to just go for it and hash it out with her to clear the air. But right now, well... you'll see. She's not her normal self and we need to keep her blood pressure down no matter what, okay?"

"Okay, Dad. I better go. I Love you," said Chastity and hung up the phone.

I took a moment to breathe before I could get my head back into the game and work mode. *Fuck this is hard!*

Kaiti's health and happiness were so fragile at the moment, and the last thing I wanted was something else to stress her out. But until Kaiti and Chastity worked out their issues, there'd be no moving forward for any of us. *Not really.* And no one would be happy, least of all me, the damn piggy in the middle.

I walked to the door of my office and emerged once more, ready to get on with the day. Hopefully they'd be able to pull the bandage off quickly, kiss their wounds better, and make peace with one another. Then we could all move on with our lives—*properly*—as a united family.

But for now, I had to trust them and their instincts and leave the ball in their court. I could only do so much. And while they'd be on my mind, I had to focus. Axel hired me for a reason, and I didn't want to let him down. I wanted us to all get along, *and* to help take his business to the next level.

We all needed to make this work... somehow. *We just have to find the way.*

CHAPTER 12

Kaiti / Katherine

My back hurt. In truth, the aching never totally stopped. But standing on Chastity's concrete porch made that pain even more obvious. I rang the doorbell a second time, taking a breath while trying to remain calm. I wasn't upset at my daughter, and the last thing I wanted to do was piss her off after barely having spoken to her in three months.

The door opened, and my beautiful daughter was standing on the other side. "Hi, Mom."

I gulped at the emotions tightening my chest like a vise. Her belly was so much bigger than last time I'd seen her. I'd missed so much! "This is a nice area," I managed to say, glancing around. "You were lucky to be able to buy on this street." I could have slapped myself upside the head for that bullshit conversation starter, but my heart was beating too fast, and I needed to calm down before we got into any of the heavier stuff.

"We were," Chastity agreed. "Very lucky."

I glanced up at the pretty new front door, with frosted glass panels and an ornate handle. It was so Chastity that it made me ache. I'd not only missed most of her pregnancy, but I'd also simply missed her—my girl.

"Come in," Chastity offered, standing back and beckoning me inside. "We only moved in officially a few days ago, so we're not quite unpacked yet."

If I knew my daughter, the house would most likely be spotless. She'd be nesting, and without a job or school to distract her, she'd have energy galore to throw into this project. I walked in, my back aching at the movement. I kept it slow, using measured, careful footsteps. I should have brough my belt from the chiropractor, but I hadn't wanted it to draw attention to my issues. I already felt overwhelmed with my status as a geriatric pregnancy, I didn't want to feel any less capable than I already did, especially to others; especially to younger mothers like my daughter.

Dumb move.

"Are you okay, Mom?" Chastity asked suddenly.

Yep, definitely should have worn my sacroiliac belt.

"Yes, I'm fine," I answered, not wanting to rattle off my long list of ailments.

Chastity was bright and beautiful, a true model pregnant woman. "Do you want the tour?" she asked, gesturing to the hallway.

"Sure," I said, then realized I needed to unload if I was going to walk much further. "Where can I leave my bag?"

"Oh, let's go straight to the kitchen. You can put it down there." Chastity raced off like a woman with no lower back pain whatsoever, then pointed toward the most beautiful open kitchen and dining space I'd ever seen in my life.

I stared in awe. The kitchen was all white, with brass hardware and gorgeous marble with white veining. There wasn't a single thing out of place. It was simply perfect. My dream kitchen. "This is" —I coughed to clear my throat— "beautiful, Chastity."

Chastity regarded me with a look of surprise that quickly transformed into happiness. "Thanks, Mom," she said, with a huge, vibrant smile on her face. "The house needed a bit of love when we bought it. Everything was a little sad. The walls, the kitchen, the carpets. It all needed to be replaced."

Jealousy began to rear its ugly green head and made me say something much less desirable than I would have liked. "You're lucky Axel can afford to do everything all at once."

Chastity's gaze narrowed at me, but she kept her tone calm. "Yeah, I know. I can't believe this is our first house, though it could be our last, too. I can't ever imagine moving."

I couldn't believe it was their first house either. I wandered over to the windows that looked out over the huge backyard, trying to gather my thoughts. I shouldn't be jealous that Chastity didn't have to struggle as I had. I should be relieved and celebrating with her. Instead, noting the backyard was still in need of attention, I said, "You haven't done much in the way of landscaping yet." Again, I could have smacked myself in the head.

What is wrong with me?

"No, not yet," Chastity answered. "Axel wants to put in a pool."

He what?

I spun around, regretting the fast maneuver instantly when my lower back pulsed with pain in rebellion. "Well, aren't you the spoiled one?" my tone the furthest thing from playful as it could be.

Chastity leveled me with her glare. "Are you jealous, Mom?"

I crossed my arms over my chest defiantly. "Why would I be jealous?" I retorted.

Because you have everything I never did and still don't? Because you have an easy life compared to me and I don't think you'll ever appreciate the struggles we went through for you?

"You shouldn't be," Chastity said. "But I can see it in your face. So, you tell me, Mom, why would you be jealous? I know you had it tough when I was little, but your life is great now. You have Dad back *and* a new baby on the way."

I turned away, facing out toward the backyard once more. She would never understand. Never. And it irked me more than I would ever like to admit to.

Chastity walked closer. "You need to tell me, Mom. What's the real problem? Is it Axel? You hate him I suppose, because he's rich and too old for me."

I rubbed my belly in slow circles, my lips pursed as tried to think about the real reasons behind my anger. "I don't hate Axel," I said finally.

"Good," she said curtly. "Because he's wonderful to me and makes me very happy."

I know he does, but how long will it last?

When I didn't speak, Chastity continued. "Okay, so it's not Axel. It must be that you still think I've ruined my life by getting pregnant? You're assuming that I've thrown away my future because I'm not continuing on to chiropractic school anymore."

I turned around to her slowly, wanting my words to come out correctly for once. I couldn't let my pettiness or bitchy anger get the better of me. This was important. Patrick was right. This day would make or break my relationship with my daughter. "I know you haven't ruined your future, Chastity. Axel will look after you no matter what happens between you, and that sort of financial security is something I never had raising you."

She sighed. "I know that, Mom. But I didn't get pregnant on purpose to spite you or prove you wrong, and I didn't choose Axel because he's rich and I wanted to trap him or something else just as ludicrous."

Sadness swamped me like heavy, sticky sludge that wanted to pull me under. Had it really come to this? That my daughter truly believed that I thought so little of her. "I know," I whispered.

"Then what did I do wrong?" Chastity burst out. "You've barely spoken to me for six months straight and now that you're here, you still won't talk to me!"

Her voice shocked me, and I gulped as panic descended like a suffocating veil. Black spots emerged at the edges of my vision.

Damn it.

I'd felt my blood pressure begin to skyrocket with anxiety the moment I'd walked into this place, and I didn't know how to calm it down. I swayed on my feet; my sense of stability lost.

Chastity rushed forward instantly, grabbing my arm to steady me. "Mom! Are you okay?"

I nodded, but I wasn't. Not by a long shot.

"Quick. Let's get you to sit down." Chasity took my hand and led me to the couch.

I collapsed into it, breathing hard, but grateful for its soft safety cradling my sore body.

Then she ran off. "What would you like? Cold water? Orange juice?" she called back.

My head was throbbing. It felt like someone had taken a mallet to my head. I should have eaten lunch before I came, but I'd been too nervous and was worried I wouldn't keep it down. "Juice would be nice."

Chastity rushed back to the couch and handed me the glass, a look of concern painting her pretty features. "What's going on with you, Mom?" she asked.

I took the drink with two shaky hands, not wanting to spill anything on the gray and white rug beneath my feet.

Chastity moved over to the couch opposite me and sat poised, waiting for the answer and affording me time to recover a little of my strength.

I took one sip, then another, the black spots at the edges of my vision finally receding. "Lots of things are wrong with me." I sighed heavily, admitting defeat. "I'm forty-three and having my second baby. The hospital staff treat me like I'm some sort of... *oddball*, because I dared to get pregnant naturally at my age."

Charity grinned at me. "Yeah, well, I suppose most of the women who get pregnant in their forties are through IVF. You're a bit of an anomaly, or rather, a miracle, really."

I nodded. What Chastity said was true. I'd met plenty of older expectant mothers at my appointments, but all were there having gone through numerous cycles of IVF. I took another sip of juice. "I have high blood pressure, and they're pretty sure I'll get pre-eclampsia; which means they'll have to deliver the baby via c-section as soon as it gets too dangerous for the both of us." Which meant I could very well have a sick baby on my hands, and with the c-section, I'd be lucky if I could stand up afterwards to even care for my own child.

Chastity gasped. "Oh, Mom, that's terrible. I'm so sorry. How are you feeling about all that? You can talk to me," she said, ever my beautiful girl with the biggest heart and a soul full of empathy.

How do I feel? Terrible.

"I hate it," I confessed. "I was still jogging five miles a day when I was eight months pregnant with you. This one, though..." I rubbed my poor baby that wouldn't get any of the healthy exercise hormones Chastity had been lucky enough to receive. "This one is taking everything I've got, plus some."

"But is the baby healthy at the moment?" Chastity asked, her hands resting on her own bump protectively.

This one I could answer easily. "Yes," I assured her. "The doctors are happy with the baby's progress. It's just my body that's struggling. I feel like a failure."

Chastity's eyes filled with tears. "You are *not* a failure!" she answered with passion. "I'm just so sorry it's this hard for you, Mom."

"No," I said, sighing again. "I'm sorry, sweetheart. I've been so... stupid. I shouldn't have reacted the way I did when you told me you were pregnant. I was just so angry *for* you—not *at* you. I felt that you were going to miss out on so much and were making the same mistakes I did."

But she isn't. Look at the house she has. The future ahead of her.

"But I'm not, Mom," said Chasity gesturing to her new home. "Look around. *This* is my new life. A man who loves me, a new house, and baby girl who will hopefully be born in a month or so, now. I know this isn't what we planned for, but it's what I want. I have no regrets."

I nodded slowly, wanting her to understand why I'd been upset for so long. "It's not what we talked about or planned for you, but I can see how happy you are, sweetheart. And I'm sorry I couldn't be here to help you."

"I didn't need your help, Mom. I just wanted you to be happy for me, especially with my baby girl. I'm—" she stopped to swallow and gulp back her tears. "I'm so ridiculously happy I'm pregnant. I really am."

I couldn't help but smile at her words. She meant them, there was no denying that truth. "I know, sweetheart. Having a daughter, especially when you have one like I did, is a wonderful thing." When I was being honest with myself, I had to admit, raising Chastity had been the highlight of my life.

"Thanks, Mom," she said and grabbed a tissue to dab at her eyes. "Do you know what you're having, yet?"

I shook my head. "No. We decided not to find out." Despite what I'd said in the past, every time we got close to an ultrasound I was so scared for the baby's health, I couldn't bring myself to ask about the sex. It seemed so trivial when I was fearing for his or her life.

Chastity waved her dampened tissue at me like a surrender flag. "So, are we okay? I mean, can we go back to being in each other's lives? I want you to come here, and I want to be able to see you. I was to go out shopping for baby stuff and talk like we used to. I want all of it. I've missed it."

I couldn't think of anything better! "Yes. I'd like that."

"Great!" Chastity said, sniffling herself together and clapping her hands. "Are you hungry, then? I can make us something to eat." Chastity groaned as she hauled herself to her feet.

I couldn't help but laugh a little. It was still good to know I wasn't alone in the discomfort department.

CHAPTER 13
Kaiti / Katherine

I watched Chastity waddle to the kitchen. "I'm not really hungry, sweetheart," I called after her. I hadn't eaten lunch, but the sweet, cold juice was sitting nicely in my stomach, and I didn't want to push it and upset the fragile balance of my temperamental belly.

Chastity laughed. "Me, either, but my specialist is worried about my weight, so I've got to eat a bit more. The baby needs the calories," she answered as she pulled out a box of chocolates.

My mouth watered.

Temptress!

She brought them back to the couch and offered me the first choice from the box. "I know you like these," she said, waggling her eyebrows.

"Thank you," I said as I took one.

Chastity grabbed one too, then sat back down on the couch to get comfortable.

"You do look a bit thin," I said, responding to her earlier comment about the doctor's opinion. I'd been told the same thing several times, so I knew it was something the specialists worried about.

Chastity laughed. "Yeah, right. Thin? I'm huge!" She ran her hand over her belly to accentuate the curve.

I shook my head, not wanting Chastity to think that way. It was normal and healthy to put on a decent amount of weight in pregnancy. "No, darling. I mean your cheeks are sunken, and your arms seem too thin." Now that I was looking at her properly, she didn't look as well as I'd first thought. Maybe her pregnancy had been harder than Patrick had been telling me?

Men! They never ask the right questions.

Chastity sighed. "I didn't mean to lose weight. It's just been difficult to eat, and with all the stress..."

"Make sure you look after yourself," I said, the guilt hitting me like a punch to the stomach. I was a part of that stress and hated myself for it. "I'm sure the doctor is right."

Chastity popped the chocolate into her mouth and chewed. "Have you got a good doctor too? Axel said that Dad's insurance should have kicked in for you."

I nodded, hating the fact that we needed to rely on Chastity's boyfriend for our basic needs. "Yes, it did. I didn't really want to change doctors, since I liked mine. But when the pregnancy became high risk, Patrick thought it was better..." I trailed off, deciding not to go into details. He'd been right, of course. The baby's health was the most important thing, but I still missed my old doctor.

"So, you're still not happy about Dad and Axel working together?" Chastity asked unexpectedly.

"It's not that I'm not happy," I said, trying my best to focus on the positives of the situation.

"Then what is it?" Chastity asked. "It's obvious you're not happy about your health insurance, and that is certainly something I don't understand."

"It's not that I'm not grateful," I said, though I'd *always* had access to good healthcare. I was a teacher and our salary packages included health coverage.

Chastity laughed at me. "You don't look grateful, Mom. You look like that chocolate in your mouth just turned to ash and you're too polite to spit it out."

I rolled my eyes at her, then forced myself to swallow the chocolate I was still sucking on. "I can't help it."

"You can't help what?"

How did I say this without sounding like a bitch?

May as well just spit it out.

"That I don't like the way we're so entwined in each other's business all of a sudden. Patrick's boss is his best friend but could also be his son-in-law. It's just too messy. If something goes wrong between you two or those two, it's going to royally screw up everything. Not only in our personal lives, but also Axel's business, and it would destroy Patrick's confidence... just everything would fall apart." I was panting now and needed to stop and take a breath.

Chastity shifted position on the couch and rubbed her belly as if unperturbed. "And if nothing goes wrong, then Dad and Axel are both happy; and so are we."

I frowned at Chastity. She wasn't thinking about all the things that could go wrong! She needed to be realistic. And not to mention... "Axel's been too generous and it makes me uncomfortable. I don't know what to say about all the money he's been throwing at Patrick."

Chastity laughed at me. "I'm sure you had a lot to say about it at the time, Mom."

Of course, I did! "He shouldn't get preferential treatment because they're friends. That's just a recipe for disaster." I was the only one out of the lot of us that seemed to be worried about mixing family and business.

"Mom, Axel told me that he offered Dad the exact amount he would pay any executive manager. The car, the insurance, it's all standard compensation. If it's a lot more than Dad used to make? Then it only further proves that he was wasted in his former role."

I opened my mouth to respond, then realized that she had a good point. Patrick had been bored and unhappy for a long time. He'd accepted low paying roles so that he could have nights and weekends off to help raise Chastity. He'd dutifully chosen stability over climbing the corporate ladder. Maybe she was right, and it was high time Patrick stop making sacrifices so that he could become the man he should have always been.

I nodded at her. "I told him the same thing about his old job. He worked far too hard for far too little." I just hadn't realized how much more he was capable of until I saw the salary Axel had offered him. Was that really what Patrick should have been earning all this time?

Chastity glanced at the clock. "The guys won't be home for a few hours still. How about we order some take-out and watch a movie?"

Tears burned in my nose and blurred my vision. Did I want some more quality time with my daughter, like we used to have? Of course, I did! There was nothing else I wanted more in this moment than precisely that.

I blinked the tears away, a part of me feeling silly for getting so emotional. "That sounds like fun. What do you want to watch?"

Chastity waggled her eyebrows. "What about 'Father of the Bride, Part Two'?"

I laughed, assuming she was joking.

Chastity wasn't. She'd already downloaded the movie and after a few presses of the buttons on her elaborate remote control, the opening credits began to roll.

"I can't believe you had this ready to go," I said, turning in my seat to watch the beginning.

Chastity hauled herself up once more. "I've been wanting to watch this with you for months," she admitted with a smile. "Now... snacks!" She went into the kitchen and made us fresh popcorn, then grabbed a couple of bags of candy and treats. "Come sit with me, Mom. You'll be able to see the movie better."

I managed to get up and walk over to her couch, where I sat down next to my daughter and stared at the feast she'd put out in front of us.

"This is a bit decadent," I said, gesturing to the bowls of sweets.

Chastity shrugged with a wicked grin. "We both need to put weight on, Mom. So, don't hold back!" She handed me a bowl of popcorn.

I chuckled as I dug in, reveling in the saltiness after the sweetness of the chocolate.

Halfway through the movie, Chastity's phone rang.

"Oh, it's Axel. Can I pause the movie for a minute?"

"Yes! Of course." It was up to the part where the mom had to tell her pregnant daughter that she was pregnant too, and that went down famously.

"Oh, yeah... okay, no problem," she said to the father of her child.

"I'll order in extra, or are you getting food at the office? Okay. Yeah... see you later, then. Love you!" She walked back to sit on the couch, two bottles of water and some more snacks in hand.

"What was that all about?" I asked.

"Axel and his minions have to stay at the office late. Something about a Japanese deal, or something. So, he told me to go ahead and eat and he'll be home as soon as possible."

"I could stay," I said, without even thinking. "I mean... I'll check my phone, but I bet Patrick has to stay too. We could keep watching movies and hang out. You can tell me all the things I've missed these last three months?"

Chastity's smile lit up her whole face. "Oh, I'd love that. Okay! Check in with Dad, but please stay. Not that I have much to say that isn't about the house, permits, tradesmen, and color combinations. Holy moly! I had no idea there were like a *thousand* shades of white until I tried getting this house painted."

I chuckled as I grabbed my phone and sent Patrick a text.

Things are going great with Chastity. She wants me to stay as Axel is working late. So, if you want to stay late too, please do. And maybe you can come pick me up from Chastity's house when you're done?

He sent back an immediate answer.

Fantastic! Yeah, love to stay and get this knocked out. They need me. See you in a few hours, beautiful. Love you.

"I'm free to stay," I announced, putting my phone down. "Your dad's going to pick me up later."

"Great! Hey, before we finish the movie, do you want to come and see the baby's room?"

"Absolutely!" I staggered to get to my feet and waddled after my daughter.

She led me into an perfectly beautiful room fit for a princess.

"It's huge!" I exclaimed, walking into the light-filled room, drinking in all the glorious features. "Oh, Chastity, it's like a real-life fairy tale."

There was a rocking chair in one corner, a lush pink rug in the middle of the room, and a beautiful white antique crib against a wall that looked like it had a hand-painted mural set upon it. And above, an adorable, classic mobile rotated, butterflies of varying shades of pink fluttering up and down. It was just gorgeous, all of it.

What a lucky little girl my granddaughter will be!

"Thanks, Mom, I love it."

"It looks like you don't need anything at all," I said, gazing around. "What on earth could I possibly gift you?"

"I need clothes!" she said brightly. "I've only got an outfit for the hospital, and that's about it. I've been holding off on buying maternity clothes for a while."

"I'd love to take you shopping," I said as I smiled at her. "The sales assistants are going to get a kick out of us, that's for sure."

Chastity laughed. "I have no doubt! Say, do you want to see the rest of the house now while you're up?"

"I'd love to."

Chastity showed me Axel's office, the master bedroom—the third bedroom was set up as a guest suite—as well as the main bathroom.

"Your home is beautiful, sweetheart. I'm genuinely so happy for you."

Chastity glowed with every compliment I gave her.

I decided at that moment that I was going to try and make everything up to her, no matter what it took.

We chatted, ate, and laughed for hours, until I got a phone call from Patrick.

"Hey, hon," I said picking up. "Are you on your way?"

"No, I'm still at work. Has Axel gotten back yet?"

I casually tottered away from Chastity so she wouldn't be able to hear what her dad was saying. "No, it's just us here. What's going on, Patrick?"

"Okay... so basically, Axel has been chasing a project that he is super excited about and I told him it was a bad deal. We had an argument and he took off. I'm surprised he didn't go straight home."

I pressed my lips into a thin line, trying not to alert Chastity to the problem. "Do you think you made the right call?" I asked, keeping my tone as chatty as I could.

"Definitely. Axel doesn't pay me to look the other way when he's about to lose millions of dollars. I know what I've advised is right, Kaiti."

I chewed on my lower lip and snorted out my nose. I wasn't saying anything. Not a chance in hell.

"Don't say I told you so, because this is *not* the time."

"I didn't say it," I whispered to him, biting my tongue hard.

"Well, don't. I'm actually worried about him. Axel's been struggling with his new role since the manager gang arrived and I have taken *so* many of his responsibilities off him. I seriously don't think he knows how to function at work anymore. I think he feels lost and pointless within his own business."

"How can that be the problem?" I whispered again, my brows furrowing.

"Kaiti, can you just trust me on this? Axel isn't coping, and I'm worried about him. If he gets home, text me to let me know, okay?"

"Will do. And I'll stay here until you come get me anyway." I wasn't going anywhere, especially if Chastity's partner was going to come home cranky and out of sorts. I'd provide whatever kind of buffer I could if necessary.

"Okay, sweetheart. See you soon," he said before he hung up.

I took a deep, steadying breath. I'd known that Patrick working with Axel was a bad idea, but I wasn't running and ducking for cover. I'd just gotten my daughter back in my life. And come hell or highwater, I wasn't losing her again.

Not a chance!

CHAPTER 14
Kaiti / Katherine

"Oh! That's Axel!" Despite her heavily pregnant state, Chastity practically flew from the room to greet her boyfriend at the front door.

I listened hard to make sure he wasn't angry, and although I could hear an exasperated tone and a sigh here and there, nothing alarming reached my ears. Though, I was certainly ready to jump if there was.

A moment or two later, Chastity walked back into the kitchen, her large billionaire in tow.

I frowned a little at his workout attire. He didn't look like he'd come from the office. Maybe he'd gone for a run to cool off?

He nodded in greeting. "Katherine, it's nice to see you."

I smiled at him in return, noting the frown lines around his eyes that I hadn't noticed last time we'd met. Maybe Patrick was right, and Axel wasn't coping with his new role. "Are you okay, Axel?" I asked.

He frowned at me. "Why wouldn't I be?"

May as well tell him the truth. "Patrick called. He's worried about you."

Axel groaned and stomped to the fridge like a teenager caught in a lie. Maybe Chastity and he weren't as far apart in age as I thought. Axel took a sip of his beer then spoke again. "What did he say?"

"You didn't tell me Dad was worried about Axel," Chastity said, looking to me.

I kept my gaze firmly on Axel.

"I didn't want to bring this home to you," Axel told Chastity, then shook his head. "Church and State."

I almost laughed. It was such a great way of saying that he was trying to keep his work and home life separate, but when he had personal and work already thoroughly mixed, I could only imagine how it must be a difficult balance for him. And there it was. For the first time, I felt sorry for the billionaire. He couldn't fire Patrick because Chastity would hate him. And if something happened between Chastity and him, then how would he work with Patrick? What had Axel been thinking when he offered Patrick a job?

Probably that he was helping everyone, all at once.

I stood up, wanting to hug Axel for the first time ever.

"Go on," he said to me, crossing his arms over his chest in a defensive position I knew all too well. "Tell me that I made a mistake, Katherine. That I should never have hired my best friend, the man that will be my father-in-law." He took another long chug of beer, then said, "I fucked up. There you have it."

And suddenly I realized I had to undo whatever damage I'd done with Axel as well. He'd gone out on a limb to help my family, and I'd all but sat back and waited for him to fail. I was done being the bad guy. There was no joy or love to be gained from gloating or expecting the worst. My family needed my support, and I was damn well going to step up and give it to them.

I shook my head adamantly. "No, you didn't, Axel. You gave Patrick the job he needed, the job he's always wanted. He's been bored for so many years, and you—you gave him the chance to do more; to be more."

Axel looked down and ran a frazzled hand through his hair. "Katherine, that is generous of you, but it doesn't change the fact that Pat is single-handedly trying to destroy the biggest deal I've ever made. He's making me second-guess everything I've worked so hard for. It's infuriating."

My immediate reaction was that I wanted to laugh at him. Obviously, he'd never had anyone tell him 'no' before in his life. He was so used to always getting his way, that at the first sign of pushback, he was ropable. I managed to keep my laughter under wraps, but I grinned and rubbed my belly. "And?"

"What do you mean, *and*?" he fired back.

I blinked at him like he ought to have worked out what I was talking about. "I mean, Axel, he's your second in charge. He loves you more than anyone."

That was a hard thing for me to admit, and I didn't mean above Chastity or me. But when it came to non-blood family, Axel was everything to Patrick. And it was a truth I needed to start remembering.

Axel leaned forward on the counter and stared down at the white marble, his brow furrowed. "What are you trying to say, Katherine?"

"I'm saying that Patrick's intentions are only to support you; to be worth the money you pay him. If he's telling you to stop and look again, maybe you should consider heeding his warning?"

He looked up and glared at me. "Seriously? You think he knows better than me what's good for my own company?"

I didn't so much as flinch, though I knew many who would in the face of Axel's anger. Instead, I simply shrugged. "What reason would he have to want you to fail? Your company puts food on the table in our house and feeds his daughter too. And I thought you'd know him better than to think he'd be making any kind of rookie mistakes at this level, Axel. If he's getting cold feet over this deal... maybe you should check yourself."

I turned toward Chastity, feeling like now was the right time to go. I couldn't be any more succinct or honest. "It's time for me to go. Can you call your driver for me please, sweetheart?"

Axel groaned. "No, don't do that. Call Pat and ask him to come pick you up. He hasn't seen the house yet, anyway."

"You want Dad to come to the house now?" Chastity asked, biting her lip as though worried about how all this would unfold.

Axel nodded. "Yes. Tell him to come in if he wants to talk. If he doesn't, he can still pick your mom up."

"Okay. Sure," I said, and began texting Patrick to come over and have a chat with Axel.

"Are you okay?" Chastity asked Axel, reaching out for him.

"Yeah, I think so, sweetheart. Things at work have just been intense lately. I'm sorry to have brought it home." Axel reached for Chastity's belly bump affectionately, pressing his hands gently to his child. "And how's our baby today? Has she been giving you grief again?" he asked, changing the topic for the moment.

Chastity glowed with happiness. "She's fine. She's just getting too big for me to carry her around like this."

"There's not long now," he said, leaning forward to kiss Chastity on the lips.

I wandered toward the coffee table snacks, feeling strangely voyeuristic witnessing Charity and Axel like this. They actually seemed beautiful together and truly in love. It was hard for me to admit, but they made for a striking and happy couple.

My phone binged and I glanced down to see Patrick's response.

I'll be there in twenty.

I walked back to the loved-up couple. "Patrick said he'll come over and pick me up. He'll be about twenty minutes."

"Perfect timing. I can take a shower, then." Axel kissed Chastity once more. "Be back soon, sweetheart." Axel walked away looking ten years older than he was.

"Maybe Patrick has a point," I muttered mostly to myself.

"About what?" Chastity asked, scooting closer to me as we watched Axel go.

I licked my lips, suddenly feeling very parched. "Can I get a glass of water, sweetheart?"

Chastity nodded her head, then waddled off to the fridge. "Of course, Mom. But are you okay?"

"Yeah, I'm just really tired." It had been a big day. One of the biggest, yet. I sat down on one of the kitchen stools, feeling quite woozy. "Thanks." I took the bottle of water from Chastity and had a sip, the cool liquid immediately soothing.

"What were you saying before? About Dad being right?" my daughter prompted.

That's right... "Patrick said that Axel has been struggling with his new role, Like he's not sure what to do with himself since all the managers he's hired have taken away most of his responsibilities."

Chastity blinked at me.

I laughed, putting my bottle down on the counter. "Yeah, I thought the same thing at first. But as you heard, that means Axel's trying to level up on projects that are a risk. Your dad advised him that he was going to lose millions of dollars and to not go ahead with the project, and Axel basically flipped out."

Chastity ran her fingers through her long blonde hair, tugging at the tangles in an agitated manner. "So, what do I do, Mom?"

It was the first time my daughter had asked for relationship advice, and I took a moment to think on it, because I didn't want to screw this up. "I think you need to reassure him. He thinks he's failing. In our family, in his work life, and when that happens, it tends to feel like your whole world is collapsing around you."

Chastity walked over to the fridge, grabbed herself a juice, then came back to me, a newly determined look on her face. "You're right. When he comes out, I'll tell him. He should know that he's appreciated and that what he's doing is the best thing for the family."

"Not in front of me," I added quickly. "Go wait in your room for him to hop out of the shower. Some things are better said in private."

"You're right, again, Mom," she said. "Thanks." Then she hugged me and waddled off toward her master suite.

A tear slipped down my cheek and I wiped it away. I had my daughter back, and my heart ached now for all the right reasons. Alone now, I had a moment to myself. I was feeling more tired than normal, but my blood pressure felt okay. I just needed to sit down for a while. I stumbled over to the couch and leaned back on the soft cushions. "Whoa," I said, trying to relax as a bit of a head spin threw me.

When Patrick texted to say he was almost here, I didn't get up. This was Axel's show. I was just here to watch and offer support where it was needed.

The doorbell peeled, and Chastity came rushing out of her bedroom to go let her dad into the house.

I heard them chatting quietly, then the front door shut, and they both moved inside.

"Come see the baby's room," I heard Chastity call excitedly to her dad. "It's my favorite place to be in the whole house. Although, the kitchen is pretty amazing too."

Patrick walked into the kitchen where he found me sitting on the couch. "Kaiti." He reached out and helped me up. "Are you doing okay?" He rubbed his hand over the baby tenderly.

I nodded. "Yeah. I've had a good day."

Patrick leaned forward and whispered into my ear. "Well done, beautiful."

"Dad! Come see the backyard," Chastity said, drawing Patrick toward the large windows that looked out into the relatively plain yard. Chastity went on about their plans for renovating, talking animatedly.

I took a breath to steady myself. I still had one more bridge to mend. I put a hand against my lower back to try and support it, then popped my head into the master suite. "Are you still in here?" I called out.

Axel was standing in the middle of the room in a pair of relaxed blue jeans and a white shirt. "Ah, yeah, why?" he answered.

I pushed the door open and stepped inside. "You're really worried about this, aren't you?"

Axel glanced away. "Yeah, I am."

"Why?"

"Why?" he repeated. "Because everything I care about is on the line. Chastity, Pat, my whole company."

I rubbed my belly in comforting, rhythmic, circular motions. "I like your list of priorities. That's how it should be."

He frowned. "What do you mean?"

"You said, 'Chastity, Patrick, then your company.' It may have been accidental, but that's how you see it in order of importance, and that's how it should be. Your wife, or partner, your best friend, and then your job." He had his head on straight, that much was obvious. And despite everything I'd worried about and thought about Axel over the years, he loved my daughter. And that was enough.

Axel scrubbed his hands over his face. "Katherine, I—"

I took a step closer to him. Whatever he was about to say, it could wait. I had to get my words out first. "No, wait. Axel. I'm trying to pay you a compliment, not upset you. I... It's no secret I haven't always liked you."

He huffed out a laugh. "Really? No way. I never would have guessed."

"You're the sort of man who tends to chew on girls and spit them out, and I was scared for Chastity in the beginning." He opened his mouth to talk, but I spoke over the top of him. "But I was *wrong*."

Axel's jaw dropped.

"There. I said it. I was wrong. About you And about you and Chastity being together. But my daughter is the happiest I've ever seen her. You're obviously a good man, a good provider, and a great friend, or Patrick wouldn't have kept you around for a decade. And he certainly wouldn't have come around as quickly as he has about you two, either."

God, it felt good to be wrong. It had never felt so good.

Axel sighed. "Why do I feel like there's a *but* coming?"

"No buts," I said. "I just ask that you listen to Patrick the same way you have on all the other issues you two have faced. He loves you, Axel. My daughter loves you. And my granddaughter is going to love you too." I had to stop talking then, because the mere mention of my granddaughter coming into the world made tears well up in my eyes and my throat clogged up.

Axel stared at me for a long moment, then nodded once. "Thank you, Katherine."

"What are you two doing in the bedroom?" Patrick asked, his face lighting up with humor as he walked suddenly into the room with us. "If I didn't know you both so well, I might be jealous."

"You?" Chastity huffed, nudging me out of the way to go stand next to Axel. "I'd just start to worry that Axel really does have a thing for pregnant women, and it's not just me!" She laughed.

Axel wrapped his arms around our daughter. "It's just you, sweetheart. I promise."

I looked at Patrick and give him a small, approving smile. It was his turn now. I'd done all I could to put this family back together.

"Should we take this party back to the living room?" Patrick suggested.

"Sure," Axel agreed. "Want a beer?"

"Yeah, that would be great," Patrick said.

We all walked back into the living room as a family and my heart sang.

CHAPTER 15

Patrick

Axel handed me my beer, his shoulders tense.

I looked over at my beautiful women and realized we needed somewhere private to chat. I loved Kaiti and Chastity more than anything in the world, but they'd interfere—they wouldn't be able to help themselves—and this situation was ours to sort out, man to man. "Hey, how about you show me the backyard?" I suggested. "Chastity said you want to put in a pool?"

Axel's gaze flicked to the couch, then he nodded in understanding. "Yeah, that's a good idea." Axel led the way through the French doors, then shut them behind us. "There are chairs beneath the tree if you want somewhere quiet to sit," he offered.

It would be dark too, which would help both of us feel more able to speak freely. We wandered off the back porch and took a seat on either side of the massive tree in the backyard. The sun had gone down and a shroud of darkness fell around us.

I wasn't sure where to start exactly regarding the disastrous deal of Axel's, so I made small talk. "It's a beautiful house, Axel. Chastity is very lucky."

"I'm the lucky one, Pat. She's amazing."

So much for small talk.

The silence stretched, then Axel began to talk. "Pat, I'm sorry about what happened today. I behaved badly. I'm better than that. I let my temper get the better of me."

He had, but no worse than other bosses I'd had. The difference was that Axel had taken everything I'd said personally, when I was giving him my professional opinion.

I took a sip of my beer. "You might be right, you know. Working together and being family might just be too much." I hadn't thought it would be a problem initially. After all, Axel and I were friends *long* before we'd become more.

Axel shifted on the bench seat. "How do people do it, Pat? Keep everything separate."

"I don't think that's so much the key," I mused. "Some of the best teams in the world are related. Fathers and sons, or brothers, and they make it work because they're related, not in spite of it."

"What do you mean?" Axel said.

I'd been thinking about this and it made sense. "Well, our friendship makes me more honest with you, more likely to tell you the truth."

Axel didn't sound convinced. "Pat—"

He didn't get it, and I had to make him understand. All our futures relied on this moment. "No, think about it. You can hire any guy to be your second. You could pay him a fortune to bow and scrape and work his ass off. But ultimately, he doesn't care if you lose twenty million dollars. He doesn't care if your company goes ass up, because he'll just move on to the next job. But you're my *family*, Axel. Your success feeds my daughter and will pay for my granddaughter's future education. And I'll be damned if I stand by and let you make a mistake that could ruin you. I just won't do it. You can fire me at the end of the day for being a stubborn asshole who won't let you close a deal I think is shit. But I won't lie to you. I won't feed your ego. I refuse to do that, Axel." I sat back and waited to let my friend and boss digest everything I'd said. Axel was quick, but he needed a minute with this.

Then he groaned. "Do you really think it's *that* bad a deal?"

How much louder do I need to say it?

"Hell, yes! I ran the numbers. Let me show you tomorrow. If I'm wrong, you can fire me."

Axel turned to look at me in the darkness of the backyard. "I don't want to fire you, but I'm not sure I can stop myself from yelling at you if you go up against me like that in front of everyone again."

I chuckled. "Yeah? And?"

"I don't want it to be like that between us. Yelling and screaming. Feeling..."

"What? Angry?" I laughed.

"Yes!" Axel all but shouted at me.

I laughed again. Axel was my age, but he had so much to learn still. "Bud, you're my best friend. I don't care if you yell and scream or throw a chair at me. I'm going to tell you straight up what I think. It's up to you if you want someone kissing your ass or covering it. Because I'm only here to do one of those things."

I'd never lie to him. I wasn't built that way. It was probably why I'd stayed in low paying, low responsibility jobs for so long. I wouldn't kiss ass to get ahead. And I certainly wouldn't stay quiet while my bosses got screwed over, or they tried to screw over someone else. It just wasn't in my nature. And with Axel I had the chance to be me and support his success... If he'd let me.

Axel stood up, then extended his hand for me to shake. "So, you'll keep working for me?"

I reached out and shook his hand.

Then my best friend pulled me to my feet.

"Yes. But *only* if you can handle me giving you the truth, because I'm not going to lie to you, Axel. Not for any amount of money."

Axel pulled me in for a brief hug. "You're a good friend, Pat."

I pulled back and gave him a friendly knock to the shoulder. "And you're a great boss, Axel. But you need to learn to take advice."

We turned and walked back toward the house.

Axel huffed out a laugh. "Yeah, I know I do. And I could probably use a little more."

We stood on the porch, shoulder to shoulder, side by side.

Our women were inside, bathed in light and laughing with happiness.

Axel wasn't moving to go inside and fell silent.

"Tell me what you need."

"I need to... slow down, Pat, but I don't know how. I hired the terrifying trio to take my workload down a notch, then got you to take the rest of the stress. But Cheryl started funneling these new projects to me and I saw the potential for growth and..."

I shrugged. "You can't stop. You're a workaholic. I've always said it."

It was Axel's turn to punch me in the shoulder. "Shut up. I need help, not your shit."

I laughed loudly. He did really need a break. "Look, you need a vacation, friend. It's obvious as the day is long. You're about to have a baby and you're killing yourself for what... another million? Please! Take Chastity away to Hawaii or something. Get some rest, smarten up that tan, and I promise your empire will still be here and standing when you get back."

Axel scrubbed his hands over his face. "Fuck, Pat. How have you done this for so many years? Managed a kid and work?"

I laughed and shook my head. "I never managed an entire company the way you do, but yeah, it's fucking hard, man. Now, you tell Chastity you're going to take her for a vacation, and I'll convince Cheryl to back off for a few years until my granddaughter is old enough." I opened the door for my friend and that's when I heard a pained moan and a frightened shout.

"Dad! Quick!" It was Chastity.

I ran for Kaiti.

She was lying on the couch, on her side, clutching at her belly.

"My love! What happened?" I asked, giving her my entire focus.

"Something's wrong!" Kaiti cried; her face red as a beet. "The baby!"

"I'm calling an ambulance!" Axel called and walked away, already on it.

I kneeled down on the rug and put my hands on my woman. "It's going to be okay, beautiful. Help is coming, just hold on."

The kick of dread had my gut churning, but I kept my gaze fixed on the mother of my child.

Katherine began to scream.

I lifted her dress to check for any bleeding but found nothing. "Just hold on, honey. There's no blood. We're going to get you through this."

She was writhing like she had when she was in the late stages of labor with Chastity, but she wasn't having the baby, so what was happening?

"The baby," Kaiti was sobbing. "The baby!"

Our baby was almost thirty weeks. He or she could survive if they had to come out now. But if it didn't... I wasn't sure how *Kaiti* would survive it. I stubbornly shut down the voices inside my head and focused on what we would need. "Chastity, get your mom's bag. We'll need to take everything with us."

Kaiti writhed on the couch, her face pale and stricken.

I grabbed her hand. "Hold on tight, baby. I'm not leaving you," I promised her. "Axel!" I called. "Go open the front door for the ambulance crew."

Axel ran off instantly.

And Chastity came back with Kaiti's bag. "I think this is it, Dad."

Kaiti let out a scream, then clutched her belly hard, an expression of utmost agony twisting her face.

My heart sank and my world shrank down to my ex-wife, my Katherine.

Oh, please, God. Just don't take Kaiti from me. I just got her back. Please.

"They're here!" Axel called out and there were sounds of commotion at the front door.

"Help is here," I crooned to Kaiti. "Hold on, sweetheart. Just hold on."

"But the baby..." Kaiti groaned.

"Just hold on, please, Kaiti." I almost sobbed but swallowed the fear down, staying as strong as I could for her. "Let's go."

Two men walked in with a gurney, and within moments had Kaiti strapped to the mobile bed and we were moving.

"Mom!" Chastity cried out after her. "We'll come in our car behind you!"

Kaiti shook her head through the pain. "No. Stay here. Rest," she commanded, still thinking about her daughter's safety and wellbeing.

Chastity looked at me, frozen by indecision.

"I'll call you with news, okay?" I said.

Then we ran out of Chastity's new house and into the white emergency vehicle.

"How far along is she?" one of the paramedic asked.

"Twenty-nine weeks, I think," I answered.

Katherine nodded vehemently behind the oxygen mask they'd put on her.

The paramedic banged on the roof and the back doors shut, then we took off.

I sat still, holding Kaiti's hand as the man examined her. There was blood between her thighs now, staining through her skirt. I stared down at my girl, smiling with all the love I had for her. "I love you, sweetheart, never forget that."

She nodded, seeming to be in less pain now.

"We're almost there." It was the longest few minutes of my life as we raced through traffic and were whisked into the Emergency Department.

They took Kaiti into a private room and got the ultrasound out straight away.

"There's the heartbeat. The baby's still with us," the doctor said with a smile.

I grabbed Kaiti's hand as tears of relief ran down her face.

"So, what is this?" I asked.

"I'll run some tests, but I'd say this was an early false labor. Your blood pressure is sky-high, Katherine."

She glared at her doctor as if he were an idiot. "Of course, it is! That was *horrible*."

"Let's see what we can do to help you and this baby get closer to term, okay? If you were closer to thirty-four weeks, I'd consider going in to deliver now, but at thirty weeks it's risky. So, let's get you hydrated, on some steroids to help the baby's lungs develop, and go from there, okay?"

The tests took hours, but in the end, the diagnosis was a lot better than expected.

When Kaiti was resting and comfortable, I gave her a kiss on the head. "I'll go and call Chastity now, all right? She has to be worried sick."

Kaiti nodded, her eyes closed as she dozed in and out with fatigue. "Yes. Please, Patrick. Thank you."

I walked out into the hall and down to the small kitchen that patient families used. There, I called Axel's phone.

"Pat! What's happened?"

I sighed. "Well..."

"Hey, let me put you on speaker."

I waited a moment.

"Is everything okay?" he asked.

"How's Mom? And how's the baby?" Chastity called out.

"They're fine," I assured them. "They're both fine," I said, making sure to get that message across straight away. I didn't want Chastity freaking out and triggering a false labor or something, too! I'd never felt so relieved in all my life. My woman was all right and our miracle baby was still with us. What greater gift could there be?

"Oh, thank God," Chastity said. "What happened, Dad?"

"It's false labor, they think. The baby isn't doing so well, and Kaiti has pre-eclampsia, which we already knew was going to be a risk. But Kaiti's only just shy of thirty weeks, so they're going to try and keep the baby in there as long as possible. They're currently giving her steroids to help the baby's lungs develop faster." Hopefully the baby would stay in there another month or even more.

"What does that mean? Is she going home?" Chastity asked hopefully.

"No. They're going to keep her in here, on bed rest. They're focusing on keeping her hydrated, monitoring the baby, as well as Kaiti's blood pressure. If anything happens and she gets worse... well..."

"Well, what? What are they going to do?" Chastity demanded with an edge in her voice.

I hated talking to my pregnant daughter about this. I didn't want her worried, or stressed, but she needed to know. "They said they'll do an emergency C-section and deliver the baby." It was not the birth Kaiti had looked forward to, but taking my woman home alive was the only thing *I* was concerned about.

"But she's only thirty weeks," Chastity whispered, obviously on the verge of tears.

I hardened my resolve. "Yeah, but your mom's strong. And thanks to the health insurance Axel gave us when I took the job, the hospital said they can keep her in and look after her until she delivers; whether that's tomorrow or in two months' time."

"Then I suppose Axel's job did come in handy, Dad."

I chuckled, deciding to share our big news, though it was meant to be something Kaiti and I told them together. "It's come in *more* than handy, sweetheart. We bought a new house a month back, thanks to this job. I can finally give your mom the family home she's always wanted. So, yeah, I owe Axel more than he knows. Which, by the way, friend, if you're still listening, is more proof why I'd never lie to you or mislead you. I would never have been able to afford the house we wanted on my old salary, and my old health insurance would never have covered Kaiti's condition. So, thank you."

There was a long silence, then Axel coughed to clear his throat. "Yeah, of course. No problem, Pat. Let's talk about it when you come back to work. Take a few days off if you need to."

"No need," I answered. "I have to go home and pack a bag for Kaiti, then I'm on my own until they call me. I'll go crazy waiting at home, and Kaiti doesn't want me in the hospital twenty-four-seven anyway, so I'll see you tomorrow."

Axel coughed again, clearly distressed in his own way. "Send Katherine our best wishes, Pat. I hope everything's okay."

"Yeah, me too. All right, I better go. I've got to get Kaiti her hospital bag from home. Luckily the both of us, she'd already packed it. I'll see you tomorrow. Bye, Chastity, sweetheart. Try not to stress. We love you," I added, addressing my daughter.

"We love you too," Chastity said, sounding teary, and speaking for them both.

Exhaling deeply, I hung up, my heart aching and overflowing with emotion.

CHAPTER 16
Kaiti / Katherine

I called Patrick around noon, sick to death of all the blood tests and nurses buzzing in and out.

"Hey, hon. How's everything going?" he asked as soon as he answered.

I groaned. "I don't think I'll have any blood left after all these tests!"

He laughed, a sound I needed in my life. "Yeah... I can imagine. But as long as you and my baby are healthy, I'm still smiling."

"Yeah, well you're not the human pin cushion!" I bitched, though I begrudgingly agreed. As long as the baby was healthy, they could run any test they damn well wanted to.

"True!" he commiserated. "Have you spoken to Chastity at all, today?"

"Yeah, she messaged me this morning before they got on the plane." Our lucky daughter was off to sunny Cancun on a babymoon, whereas my only view for the next month would be the white walls of the hospital. I sighed, feeling just a touch sorry for myself.

"It's weird to think that you might give birth before Chastity now, isn't it?" Patrick said.

I froze. "I hadn't really thought about that. She's four weeks ahead, so I'd always just assumed..."

"That she'd give birth a month earlier than you? But with our baby being a bit ahead of schedule now, you could give birth first."

"Give birth..." I muttered. I didn't want a bloody C-section, and I'd made that abundantly clear from the beginning.

"Have you tried talking to the doctor about the possibility of a natural birth with all the complications?" Patrick asked.

I sighed heavily again. "She doesn't think it's possible, and I'm just angry and disappointed," I admitted honestly.

"Sweetheart, this pregnancy was unexpected and a total miracle. What happened to going with the flow and just trusting the universe or whatever it was you were talking about the other day?"

I rolled my eyes at his far too positive attitude. "Yeah, yeah, yeah."

"Why don't you call your other doctor and have a chat with her? See what she thinks about the situation? It can't hurt to get a second opinion."

I shifted in the crisp, white hospital sheets. "Do you think I should?"

"Absolutely! I'm sure she wouldn't mind giving you her opinion, and even if she does, use your credit card, honey. Your piece of mind is worth more than money."

Tears filled my eyes. "Oh my God, I love you." I almost sobbed with the intensity of the feelings wracking me. This man *got* me, and I couldn't believe we'd found each other again.

Patrick chuckled. "You okay over there, sweetheart?"

"Yeah, of course," I managed to say, waving my hand in front of my face to dry the tears. "I'm just so happy we found each other again, that's all." There... I'd said it, but I was fighting tears again, so I forced myself to slow breaths and reached for the tissues.

"I'm going to pop by after work with paint samples and some house magazines for you to look at, okay?"

I dabbed at my face, narrowing my eyes at the phone. "What do you mean?"

"I mean... our new house needs some work. And since we aren't selling your house, why don't we do some renovations before we move in? You choose the colors and cabinets, or whatever, and Cheryl said she'll organize everything."

"Cheryl? She's Axel executive assistant, yeah?"

Patrick chuckled good naturedly. "She's more like his boss and his mom all rolled into one."

I smirked. "I like the sound of her, already."

"She's great, and you definitely have to meet her, but another time."

"How old is she?" I asked, a stab of jealousy hitting me. It wasn't often Patrick spoke about another woman in such warm terms.

"Ah... I don't know," he whispered. "Sixty, maybe?"

I couldn't help but smile now. "Okay. I can't wait to meet her."

Anyone who bossed Axel around was worth meeting!

"I'll see you after work, sweetheart."

We hung up and I began flicking through pictures of kitchens online, on my phone. I loved the house Patrick and I had bought together. It was tired, and needed some love, but it was twice the size of my current home and had a massive backyard.

But with all the expenses of the baby and me not working, I'd been happy to wait to renovate. Though seeing Chastity's house the other night had definitely inspired me to get started in the painting department.

It would be fun to get creative again!

The fact that Patrick felt the same was awesome. And even the idea that I might get a new kitchen at some stage filled me with happiness. I found some great kitchen ideas, took some screen shots to show Patrick later, then fell asleep. By the time I'd had a short shower and rested some more, my man had arrived.

"Hey, sweetheart and baby." He kissed me on the lips, then bent down to kiss my huge belly.

The baby rolled and kicked me in the liver.

I inhaled swiftly and rubbed my belly, trying to hide the pain that was robbing me of my breath.

Patrick sat down on the chair next to mine. "Still in a lot of pain?"

I shook my head. "No... no. I'm all good."

"So, what did the doctor have to say?" he asked.

I sighed and rubbed my belly. "That the baby's growing well, my blood pressure is stabilizing, and that I need to stay in bed at least another four weeks."

Patrick waggled his eyebrows at me. "Pity we can't take advantage of you being on your back for a month."

I groaned and covered my face. "How can you even *think* about having sex with me when I look like this?"

I'd never been vain enough to think I was hot or even beautiful. But I used what I had, was pretty good at make-up, and kept trim with careful eating and exercise. But that was in the past. Right now, I was pale and had huge black smudges under my eyes. I was the size of a whale and couldn't think of anything worse than something else filling up more of my body.

Patrick just grinned at me. "Sweetheart, I love you. And making love to you is the highlight of my life."

My heart broke in the strangest way. I was filled with happiness and yet felt empty. In a sad way. "I didn't think..." I swallowed hard. "You must be missing sex, full stop. It hasn't exactly been an amazing six months for you either." I licked my lips, wondering within my own mind just how far I'd go to make Patrick happy. To keep him satisfied. "Maybe. I don't know. We could, or you could..."

He waited with a big grin on his face. "I could what?"

I didn't want to say it out loud, let alone think about it. The very idea of Patrick with another woman made me want to burst into tears, but what wouldn't I do to make this man happy? To keep him mine? Especially, since I'd be out of action for another month or two. Maybe even three? Who could tell at this point? I straightened up in bed and looked him in the eye. "Maybe you could ring up an old booty call, or something if you need release? I'm not sure how you used to organize your Little Black Book, but perhaps there's someone who won't get too attached? Just for a few months?"

Part of me wanted to die on the spot for saying such a thing, but the other part was impressed with how calm and mature I sounded. What was two months of letting Patrick find physical release with another woman, compared to a lifetime of love with him?

Not to mention his baby.

Patrick stared at me, then he began to laugh.

"It's not funny," I said, whacking him in the arm with a frown. "I'm being serious!"

"I can tell you're serious," he managed to say in between his chortling. "I just can't believe you're offering for me to, or allowing me to... what? Go fuck someone else? No way, lady. That's not going to happen."

His immediate response made me smile, though I was still trying to be serious. "Patrick, I know you love me, and I want you to know how much I love you too; how much I appreciate your support. But I won't be able to service you for at least a few more months and—"

"Service me?" Patrick interrupted me, his tone bordering on exasperation now. "Honey, I'm not a fucking racehorse. I don't need a woman to *service* me. If I need any help, I've always got Mrs. Palmer on speed dial, and she's right here." He held up his hand and wiggled his fingers cheekily.

I couldn't help but laugh at how candid he was being. "Thanks, honey, but I really *am* being serious."

"And I love you all the more for it but look... listen." He reached out for my hand and squeezed my fingers tightly. "I had twenty years of screwing around with women I didn't care about. It was lonely and tiresome, and just... I can't ever go back to it. I *won't* go back to that. It's either you or nobody. Got it?"

I nodded slowly, staring down at the way our hands were intertwined. I never wanted to let go.

"I'm serious about this, Kaiti. I don't care if it's another year before you feel well enough to have sex again. I'll cope. I might go for a few more runs than normal to let off some steam, but I'll deal. I *love* you, and I'm committed to you and only you. Forever."

I glanced up at him, hearing the truthful ring of promise in his words. "Do you mean it?" I whispered, my voice wobbling.

He nodded solemnly. "I do. Now and forever."

Tears burned in my eyes as I was assaulted by memory. *'Now and forever'*. Part of his personalized wedding vows to me so long ago. I leaned forward and moaned as he kissed my lips.

Now and forever. Always.

CHAPTER 17

Kaiti / Katherine

The conversation with my old doctor went so well that she popped in to see me the following day. She totally agreed with all the medical advice I'd already been given in the hospital and was glad to see I was resting, and the baby was thriving.

While I wasn't totally happy to hear her advice, the relief it gave me was truly tangible. That peace of mind was all I'd needed, and she gave it to me. The course I was on was the right one and knowing that made me feel like I was definitely receiving the best care possible.

~

I was reading a homes and kitchens magazine and getting lots of expensive ideas for the new house, when I heard the most amazing sound.

"Mom!" Chastity cried, rushing into the room, Axel not far behind her. She leaned over me for a spectacularly wonderful and awkward hug.

I sat up to embrace her. Chastity's belly was big and pressed against mine, making the baby squirm as I was more than a little uncomfortable in this position, but I also didn't want to stop hugging my beautiful girl either. "So, tell me all about it! How was your vacation?" I asked.

Chastity stepped back, looking tanned, healthy, and happy.

A flash of blinding light caught my eye, and I grabbed Chastity's left hand, staring at the most beautiful engagement ring I'd ever seen. "Is that what I think it is?" I gasped, my eyes wide.

Chastity's face lit up with pure happiness. "Yes! Axel proposed on the trip and I wanted to tell you and Dad in person," she said excitedly.

Patrick would be sad he'd missed the initial announcement, but he wouldn't be far away.

I rubbed the sides of my belly, not quite sure how I felt, but with grim determination I forced myself to be happy for my daughter. I wouldn't make the mistake of not supporting her again. "Congratulations to both of you," I said. "You look very happy."

Axel walked closer and smiled down at me. "We are. Thank you, Katherine. But how are you doing? That's why we're here, after all."

I waved my hand through the air dismissively. "Oh, don't worry about me. I have a hundred doctors and nurses fluffing around to make sure I stay on my ass and don't move. At this rate, I'll be three hundred pounds by the time I deliver!"

Chastity reached out for my arm and gave it a gentle squeeze. "Actually, Mom, you look like you've lost some weight," she observed gingerly, as if expecting my temper to flare.

I groaned. She was right, but I couldn't eat any more than I already was. Every single bite was a strain and a test of my willpower. "It's the medication, honestly. It keeps the fluid down. I'd gotten really puffy for a while there." I patted my cheeks to emphasize my point.

Chastity and Axel glanced at each other, sharing one of those worried looks I was far too familiar with now.

Chastity sat in Patrick's chair, her hands automatically going to her large belly.

"We should have organized a photo shoot for you two," Axel said suddenly. "Both of you pregnant at the same time. What an amazing memory it would have been."

Chastity laughed and looked at me. "Oh, yeah. Just imagine that, Mom."

I almost laughed too, until I realized something quite shocking. "I don't think I have any photos of this pregnancy at all. None. I had a ton of me when I was pregnant with Chastity, but things haven't really gone to plan this time around."

How was that even possible? Surely, I'd taken one for my mom or we'd gone to an event where a photo had been snapped? But the more I thought about it, the more it became apparent that I had avoided cameras like the plague since becoming pregnant and in the very same breath I knew I'd live to regret it.

Axel pulled his cell phone out of his pocket. "Do you want one now? I can take a few pictures. Or I can arrange a photographer. They can come here if you want?"

No. That wouldn't work. I could be taken into surgery tonight to have this baby pulled out of me tonight for all I knew. Every hour was as uncertain as the next at this point in time. We had to take a picture now. After all, how often would a pregnant mother have a photo beside her pregnant daughter?

But first, I had to stand up. I threw back the blankets and slowly moved my legs to the side of the bed. "Now, here, please. In front of that plant in the corner." I pointed over near the hospital window. I liked the little bit of greenery and the sunshine in that spot, with the plain white wall and that backdrop, it could almost be anywhere.

"Okay," Chastity agreed, waddling with me to the corner.

"I like this color on you," I said to Chastity, motioning to her pink dress. It was a gorgeous baby doll style that hugged her belly and fell elegantly from her bust, and making her look beautifully radiant.

"Thanks, Mom." Chastity glanced over at Axel with a smile.

My heart was thumping in my chest, and I could see spots at the edge of my vision. But I forced the panic down and took deep steadying breaths. I would *not* pass out until this damn photo was taken. I wanted this memory. I stood beside my daughter, side by side, smiling at Axel as brightly as I could.

He took a photo then said, "Can you stand facing one another, too, so we can get the bellies?"

Chastity laughed happily and turned toward me.

I needed to do the same, though my pelvis ached standing like this. I turned to face Chastity, our big, swollen bellies touching one another.

"Smile!" Axel said.

I did my best, but I was beginning to feel faint and felt myself swaying.

Thankfully Axel was able to get the shot and rushed in to grab my hand. "I think it's time to get back into bed," he suggested.

I let him help me back to the safety of my hospital bed, my heart still racing in my chest.

Patrick walked through the door, coming straight toward me with a worried look on his face. "What happened?" he asked.

"I don't know," Axel said. "She stood up to have a photo with Chastity, then she went pale."

Patrick reached for the nurse's call button. "You know you're not supposed to get up, beautiful."

She sighed. "I still go to the toilet and shower myself, you know."

"From the looks of it, sweetheart, you may not even be doing that much for much longer. You're almost as pale as the sheets around you."

The nurse came in, answering the call.

We gave her the short version of what happened.

"Let me check your blood pressure," the nurse said, then shook her head after a minute. "Your blood pressure is far too low."

"Yeah, those stupid meds are working *too* well," Katherine grumbled. "Pre-eclampsia is supposed to have me fainting from high blood pressure, not the other way around!"

The nurse made a note on her chart. "I'm going to talk to the doctor. I'll be back as soon as I can." She excused herself and left.

Patrick sighed and visibly shook himself. "Okay... so, how are you two? How was the vacation?" he asked.

"Amazing," Chastity said, then stepped forward, arm extended, she wiggled her fingers. "And *look*."

Patrick took her hand and stared down at the stunning ring.

"Congratulations," he said and reached out to shake Axel's hand like a totally normal person and not an overprotective and pissy father.

He handled that better than expected.

"Thanks," said Axel.

"Do you have a wedding date set?" Patrick asked them and sat down beside me.

Chastity shrugged. "No idea, honestly," she admitted. "I'm just enjoying the moment and being engaged is awesome!"

Axel smiled. "We haven't talked about it, but I'd like to get married as soon as possible. So, it really just depends on if you want a maternity wedding dress or not, sweetheart?"

I could have laughed at the look of surprise on Chastity's face.

"You want to get married in the next four weeks?" she gasped.

Axel thrust his hands into his pockets. "I'd marry you tomorrow, if you'd let me."

Oh my God.

I groaned and shook my head, exchanging a look with Patrick. "Seriously! These two are nauseating." Talk about two teenagers in love.

Axel laughed. "I'm sure you two are just as bad in private."

I met Patrick's gaze. We were much more private about our affection, but Axel was right. My love for Patrick was just as strong, if not more. Patrick and I had a much longer history together than these two new lovebirds.

Axel reached for Chastity. "So? What do you say?"

"What do I say to what?"

"How do you feel about getting married sooner rather than later."

Her eyes widened. "You were serious?"

"Of course, I was. But I totally understand if you want to wait until after the baby is born."

Chastity grinned. "She'd be an adorable flower girl," she conceded.

Now that would be cute!

"She would," Axel agreed, then walked away to the far corner of the room.

"Are you okay?" she called out to him, one brow crooked.

He nodded and casually changed the subject, but it was obvious he was upset about something. "How's work been, Pat? Now that we're back, if you need time off..."

"No. It's fine for the moment." Patrick reached onto the bed and grabbed my hand. "I think I'd drive Kaiti nuts if I was hanging around here all day."

"Oh, he would," I confirmed. "Believe me, he's worse than the doctors!"

Though the fact that Patrick could have time off whenever he wanted for the me and the baby was a luxury he wouldn't have ever had in the past. That was another positive tick in the 'working for Axel' box.

"Well, you're the most important thing in the world to me," Patrick said, turning toward me and pinning me down with the intensity of his stare. "And I don't know what I'd do if something happened to you."

I didn't want to cry, I didn't. Especially not in front of other people. But hot tears welled up in my eyes all the same. I wasn't sure what I'd done right to bring this beautiful man back into my life, but I thanked the Heavens for him every day.

Axel cleared his throat awkwardly. "Well, I'll be back in the office tomorrow, so if you need to leave at any time, you can."

Patrick turned away to address Axel, giving me a moment to blink the tears away and get myself together.

"You're just busting to get back to work, aren't you, buddy?" said Patrick.

Axel nodded. "Definitely."

"Did you at least take some time off while you were away on vacation?"

"I did!" I answered mock-defensively. "Ask Chastity. I barely opened my laptop."

"I don't believe it," Patrick said, sounding surprised as a smile curled his lips.

"It's true," Chastity admitted. "I was totally spoiled. We had sleep-ins and long lunches, and lots of shopping and fancy mocktails by the pool. Axel didn't work at all, really. It was wonderful."

Now, that sounds like a babymoon!

It was a pity Patrick and I hadn't had a chance to do something similar for ourselves, but as he always told me, we had the rest of our entire lives together to make up for anything we'd missed in the past.

Patrick laughed. "Well, good for you. I'm glad you had some down-time. But I know my best friend, and you'll be busting a gut to get in there tomorrow. You're the very definition of a workaholic, and I've always admired you for your drive."

"So, I'll see you tomorrow, bright and early?" asked Axel with a grin. "You will."

Chastity walked closer to the bed and reached for my hand. "Are you sure you aren't going to find out what you're having, Mom? I'd really love to go buy him or her some outfits or something!"

I shook my head. "No, no. I'm just *so* grateful to have a healthy baby still that I don't care what it is!"

"What about you, Dad?" Chastity turned to Patrick. "Surely, you want to know?"

He laughed at her and shook his head in solidarity with me. "And ruin the surprise? No, thank you."

We went on chatting, all the while Axel was noticeably quiet.

When they finally left, I turned to Patrick. "So... how do you really feel about the fact your daughter is officially engaged to your boss?"

Patrick shrugged. "It's about time, really. They have a house and a baby together. Making it official is a good thing as far as I'm concerned."

I blinked at him in genuine surprise. "I thought you'd be mad or something to be honest."

Patrick smiled at me. "Axel's totally besotted with our daughter, Kaiti. If he wants to declare that to the world with a ceremony and an expensive piece of jewelry, then let him. The baby is the true commitment. The wedding, less so, but it's nice."

Our baby twisted and turned inside my belly.

"So, this baby—to you—is more of a commitment than a marriage?"

He grinned. "Hell, yes. Of course, it is. I'd love you to be my wife again, officially, but I'm as committed as I can be, Kaiti."

I leaned forward and kissed him, not even daring to comment on the sideways marriage proposal. Once I had this baby and was well again, maybe I'd propose to him! We'd done everything else backwards. Why not that as well?

CHAPTER 18

Kaiti / Katherine

There was a knock on my hospital room door and rather than a nurse coming to check my blood pressure for the millionth time, it was my beautiful, radiant, and heavily pregnant daughter.

"Hey, sweetie!" I called out, more excited to see her than I would have thought.

"Hi, Mom. How are you doing today?" she said, all smiles.

"Not bad," I said, focusing on the positives of the day. "We've reached thirty-one weeks today, so that's *really* good. The baby is getting bigger by the minute, and the longer he or she stays in there, the better." I rubbed my belly and stared at my daughter's. It seemed somehow smaller than mine. "You're thirty-five weeks now, right?" I asked.

"Yeah. I have a check-up with my specialist tomorrow, actually." Chastity grabbed the yoga ball from the corner of the room and sat on it with a groan. "This is great," she said. "I can see why people like to sit on them during labor."

"Yeah, they are," I answered. "But what's up, honey? You look like you need to tell me something."

Chastity looked nervous and since she'd only been here last night, she obviously wanted something. She cracked up with laughter unexpectedly. "I've been considering Axel's proposal that we get married while I'm still pregnant, but there are so many things to consider and worry about, and I kind of want your advice."

I pushed myself up into a seated position so that I could give her my full attention. "What's there to worry about?"

"*You*, for one thing," she emphasized. "I need you there. I could never have my special day without you, but what if you're still in hospital?"

And I unfortunately had no way of knowing when I'd be able to leave, let alone when the baby could come home. The earlier he or she was born, the longer they'd need to stay in the hospital. I forced a smile to my face. "When were you planning on the event?"

"Well, I spoke to a wedding planner this morning who said she could throw something together in four weeks, which would make me thirty-nine weeks. I know that sounds crazy... if I were to go into labor that week, it could ruin everything."

I couldn't stop the laugher that bubbled out of me. "You don't do things by halves, do you, sweetheart?"

"Why aren't you trying to talk me out of this?" she said with a frown. "Don't you think it's insane?"

Now, I *really* couldn't stop laughing. There were tears in my eyes, and the feeling of happiness in my heart made me want to never stop.

This is the kind of joy I've been missing out on all these years...

"Mom, seriously. Do you think it's smart to throw some expensive party together the week before I'm due?"

I wiped my eyes with a tissue. "Well, you were ten days late, so you never know but you could go *way* over your due date, Chastity. Babies are unpredictable like that, and pregnancy isn't an exact science."

"Over?" she gasped, a look of instant terror in her eyes as though the idea had never occurred to her.

How does she not know this?

"Yes. A normal gestation is considered anywhere between thirty-seven to forty-two weeks," I informed her. It seemed like a serious omission by her healthcare providers if they hadn't forewarned her.

"Oh my God. Forty-two weeks! Imagine that. I'd be the size of a bloody house, Mom!"

I grinned at my gorgeous daughter, consciously choosing to get on board with her crazy.

She deserves every ounce of happiness that can be squeezed out of this situation!

"To answer your question, I do think it's insanity, but *everything* about you and Axel is insane, sweetheart. The way you fell in love around your dad, your age difference, you finishing school while dealing with all the other pressures; like your pregnancy and the house renovations. Everything has been done at lightning speed, and yet I've never seen you look so genuinely happy. And your father has said the same of Axel, too. He's never seen Axel so happy either. So, I think you should go with your instincts on this one, sweetheart. What's your heart telling you?"

Tears shimmered in her eyes. "Um... that getting married while being heavily pregnant would be amazing—like a declaration of how much we love each other—the commitment we have to being a family."

That's exactly it!

"Then do it!" I cried. I wasn't standing in the way of my daughter's happiness. Not anymore. Not ever again. She was a grown woman and deserved to be treated as one. If she knew what she wanted, then I was going to support her every step of the way! "Risk it," I told her. "If you have to cancel due to the baby or a complication, who cares? It's not like Axel can't afford the cost."

"Mom!" she glared at me.

I shrugged. "It's true!" I said. "And he won't even care. Everything can just be postponed to a month or so afterwards, anyway."

Chastity shifted on her chair, her lips twisting in thought. "But what about you? You could still be here in four weeks' time. I can't get married without you there, holding my hand. I just can't! I won't."

The words were so perfect that tears burned in my eyes once more, and I decided to share our little secret with her. "I'll be there, sweetheart, I promise. And, although he may not be able to attend in person, your little brother will be there in spirit, too."

"What?" Chastity croaked. "You're having a *boy*? I thought you didn't know!"

I wiped at the tears. "We weren't going to find out, but we've had so many scans now that it was becoming very obvious." The ultrasounds were happening almost daily at the moment, and we'd have to be blind not to notice. Patrick had asked the sonographer and it was confirmed just yesterday.

Chastity reached out and pressed her hand against my belly, something she'd never done before. "My little brother. I can't believe it, Mom."

"Your dad is so happy," I said, unable to hold my feelings inside any longer. "I just hope he's healthy. The scans all say he's big and strong, but so much can go wrong now, especially with my age. The doctors and nurses do nothing but refer to my age like it's a disease. You'd swear I was a leper or something."

"Ignore them, Mom. Your baby's a miracle. You just need to keep him in there a little longer and you're doing amazing."

I nodded, then decided to change the subject.

What will be, will be.

"Show me what dresses you're looking at. Do you have any ideas of what you want to do?"

"I do. I was thinking of something small and intimate, maybe fifty people? I found some hotels I like the look of, with great gardens for the wedding, and I did find a dress, but it is *so* expensive!"

Had she forgotten she was marrying a billionaire? "I'm sure Axel told you that you could have anything you like."

She nodded with a gleeful, but nervous grin. "He did."

"And your father will want to help with the wedding or the honeymoon. I'm not sure, but he'll want to pay for something." Even though his salary came straight from Axel's company, Patrick would definitely want to contribute.

"Thanks, Mom." She pulled out her cell phone and started scrolling. "Can I show you what I've found so far?"

I shuffled a little closer, "Definitely. Show me."

The afternoon was an absolute dream. We did nothing but talk about wedding stuff. Dresses, flowers, reception packages, and the wedding officiant. Money was no object, which made everything so much more fun than I could have ever imagined.

Chastity was too nervous to book the wedding planner, so I made the phone call for her from my hospital bed. And it went so smoothly, she asked me to make some more calls. Once again, I felt important in my daughter's life, and part of me couldn't believe this was happening. She still needed me and I couldn't even begin to describe how good that felt.

And now, I was having another baby and starting the whole cycle all over again. And why not? I'd done a good job with Chastity. She was beautiful, inside and out. So much so that a man like Axel had met her, got her pregnant and proposed to her in a matter of a few months. He was quite literally head over heels for her. He locked her in and made sure she would never get away, in the best way possible. He knew she was amazing, and I was so happy for her.

After she left, I ate dinner, had another damn blood draw, and then Patrick arrived.

"Hey, sweetie, you're looking happy," he observed.

I settled back against the pillows, exhausted to the very bone. "I am happy. Chastity came by today and we planned a lot of her wedding. We booked the planner, talked about flowers and her dress. It was fantastic. I loved it."

Patrick sat down in his chair next to me, his eyebrows high. "They're planning the wedding already?"

I laughed and rubbed my belly, loving the strong kicks that bruised me from the inside, but reassured me that our son was alive and well. "They're getting married in a month."

"They *what*?" he asked, his eyes becoming saucers.

I grinned at him. "Obviously, Chastity hasn't spoken to you just yet."

He frowned. "I had a missed call, but I wanted to get here as quickly as possible, so I didn't return it... damn."

"She'll catch you up," I said, reaching for my glass of water.

"And how are you feeling today?" Patrick asked, pulling out a protein bar, his classic pre-dinner snack.

"I'm good," I said, swallowing hard as a wave of nausea washed over me.

"You're as pale as a glass of milk and I can tell you're in pain," he countered with a grimace.

I shrugged. "So what? I'm past thirty-one weeks, and they'll go in and take the baby out soon. I'll put up with whatever I need to in order to keep him in there as long as I can." Sciatica, no sleep, headaches. I didn't care. Not today. My baby boy was healthy and my daughter was happy. I looked over at Patrick. "Honey?"

He smiled at me. "Yeah?"

"Will you marry me? Again?" I proposed.

He reached out and grabbed my hand. "Are you serious?"

I grinned at him, my heart overflowing with love. "Absolutely. I love you more than anything in the world and want nothing more than to be your wife and be a family with our baby boy."

Patrick got to his feet, cupped my face and kissed me hard.

I kissed him back, giggling when he pulled back with a big smile on his face. "So?" I asked him, "Are you saying yes?"

He shook his head. "No, I'm saying hell yes! Of course, I'll marry you, Kaiti. Tomorrow. Today. Every day!"

I grabbed his hand, my soul singing with joy. "I don't want to steal Chastity's thunder. So, please, let's keep this between us until after their wedding."

He nodded, then lifted my arm to kiss my hand. "We need to go shopping and buy you a ring."

"That sounds amazing." But honestly? I didn't care much about jewelry, although a new wedding band would be beautifully symbolic and perfect. I had Patrick, again, and God willing, soon I'd have my baby boy in my arms, too.

CHAPTER 19

Patrick

Over the next week I watched Kaiti get thinner and paler. She was also cranky as all hell yet wasn't up to her usual level of spirit. I could see my feisty woman disappearing before my very eyes.

The doctors were worried about her being able to make it much further, but Kaiti was valiantly fighting to stay in that hospital bed and out of the operating room. But the day she hit thirty-two weeks I received the phone call I'd been dreading for months.

"Patrick?" Kaiti sounded scared.

I stood up from my desk and reached for my car keys. "Yeah, beautiful? What's up?" It took every bit of my strength to stay calm in that moment. Something had changed or something was wrong, I could tell that much from the frightened quaver in her voice. Either way, Kaiti needed me. That much was certain.

"The doctors... um, they want me to go into surgery. Can you come, please?"

My heart pounded sickeningly hard against my sternum, but I forced myself to sound calm when I asked, "When? Now?" I was already walking to my office door.

"Yeah. Now."

I closed my eyes and forced my voice not to tremble. "I'm on my way, beautiful. I love you. Try and stay calm, okay? I'll be there as soon as possible."

"I love you, Patrick. Bye." Then she hung up.

I could tell she was shaking on the other end of the line, but I needed to stay cool if I was going to get to the hospital in one piece. I should have walked but instead I set off running to the front desk and whacked my hand down in a panic. "Cheryl. I've got to go. The baby—" I breathed.

"Go. I'll take care of everything." And she would. I knew she would. Cheryl was truly awesome, and when I had time to tell her, I was going to make sure she knew it.

I ran to the elevator doors, adrenaline pumping hard in my veins now. I rode it down to where my car was parked and thanked Axel once again for giving me allocated parking, even though I'd told him not to. The drive to the hospital was fucking insane. I wanted to scream at every fucking red light I copped. I almost stopped the car so that I could get out and run on three separate occassions.

But eventually, I got there in one piece and managed to get inside without tripping over or having a car accident. I was sweating when I arrived, my stomach twisting with worry as I ran into Kaiti's room. "Hey, beautiful."

There were two nurses in the room with her. "I think they want you to go put surgical stuff on," she answered.

"Yes, sir. Come with me please," a nurse who I'd never seen before said to me.

I bent down and pressed a kiss to Kaiti's lips. "I'll be with you every second, okay? Don't be scared. You've carried our baby boy all this way. It's time to let the doctors do their thing."

She nodded and cupped my face. "Okay."

I kissed her again, hard. "I love you. And I'll be back."

"I've got to call Chastity," Kaiti whispered, her eyes haunted with worry.

"Do it," I said, forcing a smile on my face. "She'll want to know. I'll go get geared up." I wanted nothing more than to scoop her up out of bed and hold her tight. But that was the last thing she needed me to do, so I turned and followed the nurse out of the room. As soon as we were out of earshot, I said to her, "What's happened? Is she in danger? Is the baby?"

The nurse led me to a room where she told me to wash my hands thoroughly and put blue scrubs over the top of my clothes.

"Tell me what's going on!" I demanded, starting to wash my hands when the nurse remained silent.

"Katherine and her baby are possibly headed for danger. Her blood test results came in this morning and the doctor wants them both out of this situation as soon as possible."

"But the baby is two months from full term," I said, my heart still thumping in my chest like a frantic bongo drum.

"He's doing very well given the situation," the nurse assured me. "He's no longer undersized, but he's showing signs of stress due to Katherine's blood pressure. He'll be safer outside the womb, now."

I didn't want to think so, but I had to trust the doctors to save my son and the woman who would be my wife once more.

Soon. Very soon.

I waited for what seemed like forever, but then was allowed into surgery.

Katherine was strapped to a table, a modesty sheet pulled up so we couldn't see what the doctors were about to do.

I rushed to her side and pressed my lips to her face. "Beautiful girl, are you okay?"

"Yeah..." She smiled at me, and it was obvious that whatever drugs they'd given her to calm her down via the IV were affecting her.

"You've done so well, sweetheart," I said, bending down to kiss her forehead, then the tip of her nose. "I truly love you, and I cannot wait to meet our son."

The surgeons were at work beyond the curtain, and I tried not to listen as they cut my beautiful woman open. They were chatting casually away about the football, then about the instruments they were using. I tried not to get angry. This was a beautiful moment for us—an important moment—and they were fucking chatting like they were having a beer at the end of the day.

"He's coming, very soon," I said to Kaiti.

Then suddenly the doctor announced that he was out. "Here's your baby," the doctor said, holding our son above the curtain, the umbilical cord still attached. He was clearly not breathing, still sleeping in a strange, purple way. But he was beautiful. And tiny.

I swallowed hard, emotion swimming up to clamp down on my throat. But I didn't get the chance to speak or touch him, he was whisked away by a nurse to be attended to, and then machines began to beep loudly all around me.

Kaiti wasn't talking anymore.

"Honey? Kaiti!" I stood up and looked around at the doctors in the room. "What's happening to her?" Panic hit me, hard.

"She's losing too much blood," a doctor said, moving quickly around the room. "Take the baby into the NICU!" he ordered.

A nurse came over to me, my son in a plastic crib, swaddled in a white blanket. "Come with me, Patrick."

"I can't leave Kaiti."

"The doctors need to concentrate, now. Please, come with me," she repeated.

I glanced back at my beautiful woman, my heart feeling like it was being physically ripped out of my chest. But they were working on her and bringing in transfusion bags, and my son needed me too. I did as I was told and went with the baby and his mobile plastic crib. "Is she going to be all right?" I asked, putting my hand on his belly, loving the warmth of him and the way he squirmed. Alive and healthy, though still tiny.

"The doctors are doing their best. We're going to take your son to the neonatal intensive care unit as he is eight weeks premature. I'll assess him there."

He was breathing on his own and looked perfect to me, but I didn't argue as I followed the nurse to the preemie station. The next hour was the longest of my life. I paced along the corridor, looking in on the special care unit and dying to go and find out about Kaiti. Was she all right? Were they stitching her up? Was she conscious again?

I tried not to think about the possible outcomes of today. Losing Kaiti was on my list of things that I would not be able to survive. But who would raise our son if I joined my Kaiti in the afterlife? Axel and

Chastity immediately came to mind. He'd have his sister, at least, and would be raised alongside his niece, with every financial advantage any parent could ever dream of.

Then it hit me. I needed to call Chastity. She'd be worried sick. She hadn't heard from either of us since her mom called her prior to the surgery. As soon as I got the report from the nurse about our son, I dashed off to get my phone from the nurse who'd taken it earlier. I dialed Chastity's number, taking my first sip of water in hours.

"Hey, Dad! Is everything okay?" she asked, sounding as breathless as I felt.

I forced a smile to my face and focused on the positives. "Yes. The baby's fine. You have a new baby brother. You're officially a big sister."

"Oh, Dad, that's so amazing! And how's the baby? How big is he?"

I smiled as I told her the news. My son was a fighter, just like his mom. "He weighs almost four pounds and he's doing very well. They've taken him straight to the NICU in case he has any issues, but the doctors said that he should only be in there for a few days, hopefully. But he's safe."

He'd been squalling and fighting when they'd measured him, and although I'd rushed straight over to make them stop, it had made me so proud to see him come out fighting.

"What about Mom?" Chastity asked. "How is she?"

I held my breath. How did I tell my daughter that I didn't actually know how her mother was, and that I was sick to my stomach with worry? "She's okay," I lied.

"What happened?" she pressed, her tone uncertain.

"Well, her blood pressure skyrocketed during surgery, and she lost a lot of blood." I winced at the thought. Or that was what I'd heard one of the doctors say, at least. "She's still in there right now. I had to come out with the baby. I wasn't given a choice."

"Um…"

I closed my eyes and shook my head. I could slap myself for calling so early! What an idiot I was. I should have waited until I knew Kaiti was fine before calling Chastity. I tried to reassure her. "She'll be okay, sweetheart. Your mother's a fighter, you know that. She's fierce. We just have to wait for her to come out of surgery."

"I'm just down the street," Chastity said. "How about I come straight to the hospital now?"

I wasn't sure what she could do, but I wasn't going to fight her on this. "If you want to," I said.

"Yes. I do."

Kaiti would be mad at me if I were to make the wrong choice here. "I don't want you to be stressed, Chastity."

"Dad, I'm going to be worried about Mom no matter what. I'd rather sit with you than worry at home."

That was a good point. "Okay, sweetheart. I'll see you soon." I hung up and sighed. How was it possible that such an incredibly beautiful day could also be the most terrifying of my entire life? The sun was shining, and the birds were singing, yet my world dangled upon the knife-edge precipice of dream or disaster. The anxiety threatened to swallow me whole. All I could do was wait, and pace, and wait some more; lost to my thoughts as I battled to keep them from turning toward darkness.

If I lose Kaiti now, I don't know what I'll do.

CHAPTER 20

Kaiti / Katherine

Our son, Grayson, was the most beautiful baby I'd ever seen, and my heart swelled with love as I gazed down upon him. "We're so lucky," I whispered to Patrick as we stood beside his incubator.

"Yes, we are," he agreed as he stared down at our tiny little miracle, our baby's small fist wrapped around Patrick's pointer finger. "Have you heard more from the doctors about when we can take him home?" he asked.

I sighed, running my fingers over the crib and wishing I could pick up my baby and hold him close to my heart. I kept having to remind myself that the doctors and nurses were keeping him healthy, not deliberately withholding my son from me. "I don't know. From the sounds of it, another couple of weeks, at least. I can go home tomorrow, but since I'll be actively pumping and bringing milk in all day, every day, I wonder if I shouldn't just stay here with the baby."

I'd breast fed Chastity until she was twelve months old, and I was determined to try and do the same for Grayson, even if he was being fed through a tube at the moment.

"Go home tomorrow?" said Patrick, his brow furrowing as he

looked up at me. "But you just had major abdominal surgery only a few days ago."

I shrugged. "That's how it is now. They want us home as soon as possible. I guess they need the beds."

Patrick's frown said it all.

"I know," I agreed. "I don't want to go home without him either." In fact, the very idea broke my heart into a million pieces. He'd been a part of me, quite literally, for so long, I couldn't imagine being so far away from him. Just being in two different rooms was difficult enough! It made my head spin.

How can I leave him?

"Well, let's pray that he improves quickly, and we can get him home as soon as possible, then," my handsome man said.

I nodded, needing to change the subject or I was going to cry again and if I did, I wasn't sure I'd be able to stop.

Damn post-pregnancy hormonal deluge!

"Speaking of home, have you heard any news on the new house?"

We were supposed to close in about two weeks, and I hadn't scheduled the painter or any of the tradesmen that we needed to work on the house before we moved in, yet.

Patrick's face lit up with a large smile. "Yes, actually. I got an email from their lawyer yesterday asking to move settlement up a week. What do you think? Do you want the keys earlier rather than later?" he asked, waggling his eyebrows at me.

I gaped at him. "Really?"

He nodded. "Yes, and I think we should do it. I mean, why not? It'll be something to look forward to after all this stress is a memory."

"When Grayson and I come home?" I asked, projecting positive thoughts forward to that perfect day.

Patrick nodded. "Yes... and I know you wanted to organize things yourself, but what do you think about hiring Chastity's decorator to do our new kitchen for us?"

I pressed my lips into a thin line. "Isn't she expensive?" We didn't have Axel's kind of money, and it seemed like a ridiculous extravagance when we had another baby to put through school now.

Patrick shrugged. "Axel said he'd pay for the designer as a baby gift. We just pay for the kitchen, labor, and appliances."

I stared down at my tiny baby boy, trying to see this as the gift it was and not let my ego get in the way. "I suppose. We don't really need anything else, do we?"

Patrick glanced up at me again and smiled. "That's my girl. No, we don't need a stroller or any of that stuff. Let Axel pay for the designer, then you'll get the kitchen of your dreams, and we can finally have the family we always wanted."

I couldn't stop the tears that welled in my eyes this time.

Damn it.

"Hey, are you okay?" he asked, his tone automatically soothing and reassuring.

I wiped at the moisture on my cheeks. "Yes. I think it's just... you know. The hormones and the all the emotions. Just everything from the last few days."

Patrick took his hand out of the incubator and reached for me. "Let's go back to your room, beautiful."

I pressed a kiss to my fingers, then to the plastic crib that was keeping me from picking my baby up. "We'll see you soon, sweetheart," I promised.

I let Patrick take me back to my room, then it was time for him to go to work. He kissed my lips and said goodbye.

Once settled, I ordered a cup of tea and rested in bed. My blood pressure was returning to normal, and although my belly was still very sore, I was feeling a lot better now that I was no longer pregnant. The sound of footsteps met my ears just as I was taking a sip of tea, then my beautiful daughter burst into my room. "Chastity," I breathed.

"Oh, Mom! You look wonderful," she said, rushing to my side.

I managed to smile at her, knowing full well that I looked anything *but* wonderful. But I was alive and so was my baby, and that's all that mattered at the end of the day; the quality of life and freedom would come in time. "I feel a little strange but there's no pain, thanks to all the meds they have me on. How are you doing, sweetheart?"

Chastity was weeks away from giving birth and she still looked as vibrant and happy as ever. "I'm good," she said, sitting in the chair next to my bed. "Your tummy is half gone and you look so good."

I ran a hand over my rapidly decreasing belly.

I miss my baby.

"I'm recovering well, so I'll be able to make your wedding in a few weeks," I told her. It was something I cleared with the doctors as soon as I could.

Chastity's eyes bulged. "Seriously? I was going to cancel it until you recovered, Mom. You know, maybe leave it until next year some time?"

"No way," I declared. "I'll be discharged soon enough, and the doctors have said the baby is doing really well. He's a true fighter. So, assuming he starts feeding properly and doesn't have jaundice, we'll both be home soon enough!" Or at least, that was my hope. No need to stress Chastity out about Grayson.

Tears shined in her eyes, a mix of joy and uncertainty. "That's too much pressure on you, Mom. You don't need to—"

I reached out to my beautiful daughter, needing to reassure her. "I want to, Chastity. Look... I know I haven't been a fan of Axel's. Right from the start, I know I was a bitch to him."

Chastity didn't respond and merely pursed her lips, maintaining her silence.

I continued. "But he's a good man, and he's good for you. I never thought I'd say this, but he deserves you, sweetheart. With all your beauty and sweetness and intelligence and heart, I wasn't sure you'd find the kind of guy that would complete you. But you have. And you both deserve to enjoy the day you planned."

Chastity stared at me, her worry clear in her eyes. "I want you there, Mom. It wouldn't be my special day without you."

I smiled at her. "I'll be there, sweetheart, I promise. And God willing, so will your brother. Even if I have to roll in via wheelchair and carry him on me." Which I wasn't above doing. The doctors could bloody join us and sit at our table if they wanted, but Grayson and I would be there with bells and whistles on for Chastity's big day.

Chastity grabbed my hand. "Please don't let it come to that."

I laughed. "I'll be there, so don't cancel anything, do you hear me?"

Even if it meant using Axel's money to make it possible, I'd do anything to make my daughter happy.

Chastity rubbed her huge belly. "It was crazy of me to even attempt a wedding this close to the end of my pregnancy, let alone yours." She was a little crazy, but I'd always loved that about my fearless daughter. She had my fiercely independent streak.

"You'll be fine," I said, as reassuringly as possible. "And I can't wait to see you walking down the aisle on your father's arm. It will be a day to remember."

"Are you really sure? I already called the wedding planner to cancel everything, but she was tied up and hasn't gotten back to me yet."

"You're not canceling anything on account of me!" I said, again, and this time I added a soft glare to add weight to my words.

"You're really, really sure?" my daughter ask, her brow furrowed in concern.

"Yes!" I said extra loud.

Chastity's phone began to ring, and she gasped. "It's the wedding planner, what do I do?"

"Well, tell her that's nothing's changed and everything is still going ahead. Then you can go see the baby."

"What did you name him?" Chastity asked as the phone continued to ring.

I leaned back on my pillow. "Grayson Patrick."

"That's beautiful, Mom. I really like it."

So do I.

"Good, I'm glad. Now answer the damn phone, sort this out, and go see him. He's beautiful."

"I will!" she sang out to me as put the phone to her ear, practically running from the room.

I closed my eyes, trying to conserve my strength. I had a wedding date to aim for now. And I wasn't going to miss it for the world. I'd call in a mobile medical unit to attend the ceremony if necessary. I already knew Axel would be the first to agree to it. He wanted to marry Chastity as soon as possible, and if me being there made it happen, he'd make it rain dollars! And for perhaps only the third time since accepting Axel into our family, I was wholeheartedly grateful that he was a hard-working billionaire.

One way or another, we'd make sure Chastity got the glowing, fully preggers wedding of her dreams.

I owe her that much.

CHAPTER 21

Kaiti / Katherine

Two weeks after Grayson was born, Chastity's wedding day arrived. Amazingly, she was still pregnant, but getting grumpier by the day. Even so, I couldn't be happier for my first born. She was going to have the wedding of her dreams, to a man who absolutely worshipped the ground she walked on.

As long as my granddaughter could wait eighteen more hours before she was decided to make her grand entrance into the world, it would truly be the perfect day.

Axel had shown his generous nature and surprised me yet again when he literally paid for us all—every single wedding guest—to stay in the hotel where they were getting married. It was a beautiful gesture and it meant no one would have to drive, and everyone would be safe and sound after a day and night of blissful festivities. He really was a gentleman, and I realized that despite the closeness of our ages and the social awkwardness that presented, I'd actually be proud to call him my Son-In-Law.

As fate would have it, I'd woken up more than a dozen times, afraid I'd accidentally sleep in. So, in true mommy delight, I spent most of the night attending to my beautiful son, who'd just been allowed to leave the hospital yesterday. When I finally awoke to the sight of warm sunshine streaming in through the half open curtains, I sat bolt upright —instant panic in my heart—and glanced over at my still sleeping man. "It's morning! We have to get up!"

Patrick groaned from the mattress beside me. "Are you sure? Because I'm pretty sure you've said that at least ten times since we went to bed."

I actually laughed at the father of my children and rolled carefully out of bed. Grayson, thankfully, didn't stir. He was swaddled up and sound asleep in his bedside bassinet. "I'm off for a shower," I whispered. "What time do you have to go see Axel?"

Patrick crawled over to my side of the bed, so he could be closer to Grayson. "Not until... ages away. I'm going back to sleep," he mumbled.

I left Mr. Grouchy and went to take a long shower to wash my hair. My stitches were almost completely dissolved, and although there was still some pain and tenderness with certain movements, I was almost back to my old self, which was a miracle in itself.

I glanced at the mirror, grimacing at my belly and its numerous stretch marks, then turned away and grabbed a towel. I wasn't going to let myself have a single negative thought today. Not about my body, Axel, or anything to do with the wedding. Today was going to be perfect and I was all about maintaining the good vibes.

I was going to get styled with Chastity, so I clipped up my wet hair and dried my body. I slipped into a soft gray dress and walked back into the bedroom where Grayson was just beginning to stir.

"Good morning, baby boy," I cooed at him, loving the way his little face screwed up in hunger and the way he arched his back to stretch out his little body.

"Let me get him," Patrick said, reaching into the bassinet to pick up our son.

I glared at him. "He barely weighs five pounds." Which was an amazing weight gain from his birth. I was so proud of him and his progress.

"And you're not supposed to be lifting him yet, so sit. Do you want to feed him before you go to Chastity's room?"

I nodded and moved around the bed to settle on the other side of Patrick, my back against the headboard.

Patrick held Grayson with two hands, kissing him softly on the head.

"You're already so in love with him, aren't you?" I asked him. A rather rhetorical question at this point, but still, I liked hearing him talk about how much he loved our little family.

Patrick grinned at me. "Well... I love him with all my heart, but I'm *in* love with you."

I leaned forward and kissed him on the lips. "I love you, too, Patrick."

Patrick put Grayson carefully into my arms as if it was the most natural thing in the world, like there wasn't over two decades between our babies.

I moved my dress aside to breastfeed our bub. He was still being mixed fed, sometimes bottles of formula and sometimes from me. But considering he was eight weeks premature; his suckling reflex was developing very well. Once he'd had a good drink, I lifted him up onto my shoulder and rubbed his back, helping him to shift any wind that may be causing him discomfort. "I'm dying to go and see Chastity," I said. "Would you mind if I go when we're done here?"

Patrick rolled out of bed, then reached for the baby. "Not at all."

I got up off the mattress once more, tucked my breast away, then grabbed the baby wrap. "I'll just change him, then go."

Chastity's room was just down the hall, so it wasn't far to go. Even so, I was nervous and excited all at once. I changed Grayson's diaper, happy to see that his belly button was cleaning up well since his umbilical cord stump fell off a few days ago.

"We'll see you later," I told Patrick, grabbing one of the room keys and sliding Grayson into the baby carrier that meant he was held warm and snugly against my body like a little baby bear.

Patrick kissed me again and walked me to the door. "When are we going to tell Chastity that we're getting married again?" he asked, obviously excited to make it official.

I rolled my eyes and grinned playfully at him. "Well, not today, *obviously*."

It was his turn to roll his eyes. "I know that. I'm not totally daft. But when?" he pressed.

I took a moment to think about it. "Well, maybe sometime after their baby is born? I don't want to take away from any of Chastity's experiences at this point. She deserves all the light to shine down on her."

Patrick kissed me again. "Since when did you get so selfless, huh?"

"Hey!" I complained, elbowing him in the belly.

Patrick laughed. "Ease up! Go on, go enjoy your morning with our daughter, and I'll see you at the ceremony, beautiful."

I nodded and headed down the brightly lit hallway to Chastity's room. That's where I ran into Axel, obviously heading for the gym.

"Morning!" he called, pulling a key card from his pocket. "I was just coming to drop this off to you in case you wanted to get in and see Chastity."

"You're a mind reader," I said, taking the card from him. "Thank you."

Axel nodded, then grinned. "Well, I'm headed to work off some damn nervous energy. See you later?"

"Yep," I said. "We'll be there with bells on."

"We wouldn't have had it any other way," Axel said with a tender smile I'd only ever seen him direct toward Chastity.

We stood there, staring at each other for a minute, smiling, a sense of family flowing between us. Finally, everything was at peace between he and I.

"Well, anyway. See you later," he said with a grin, and headed off.

I watched him go, shaking my head. If anyone had asked me what sort of man Chastity would marry, a man twice her age would not have been at the top of the list, and yet here we were. And Chastity had never been so happy. It was funny how the most unexpected could be *exactly* what was needed. I tapped the cardkey against the door pad and pushed on the handle.

The suite Chastity had was very similar to ours, with a huge bed and a sitting room. I picked up the phone and called down to room service, ordering several breakfast items and drinks. I was starving, and Chastity would need food to get her going for the day, whether she wanted it or not; she'd need the energy and the baby needed food, too.

Once I finished speaking to the woman on the phone, I hung up and walked through the apartment, not finding her anywhere I could see. I walked into her bedroom, where the duvet was thrown back, but my pregnant daughter was missing.

"Chastity? Are you awake yet?" I called out, not wanting to scare her if she came out of somewhere unexpectedly.

"Yeah, Mom!" she called back. "Just in the bathroom." She opened the door to the ensuite and waddled out in a big fluffy and luxurious bathrobe.

I clapped my hands together in glee. "I've ordered some room service, so breakfast should be here soon. Then the hairdresser and makeup artist will arrive. It's all systems go!"

Chastity sat down in a large armchair; her eyebrows knitted together in a suspicious frown. "How come you're all bouncy already, Mom? It's a bit early isn't it?"

I laughed. "Well, it is my only daughter's wedding day!" And as I was no longer pregnant, I felt *so* much better than I had a month ago. A feeling Chastity would experience soon enough.

"Yeah, but you had major surgery a few weeks ago, and you look amazing!"

I smiled at her, knowing I didn't look amazing, but all the same I was sticking to my personal pact to refuse all negativity today. "Your dad's been looking after me at home, and I've been lucky with my recovery. I feel so much better than I did while I was pregnant, so even with the pain, my body is rebuilding." I rubbed my hands absently over Grayson's back, loving the ability to hold him without upsetting my stitches.

Chastity leaned back in her chair with a sigh. "I can't wait for this baby to come out now, to be honest. Last week I wasn't really feeling it, but today... I'm done."

I grinned at her. If she was feeling that way, it wouldn't be long now. "You only need to make it through today, then my granddaughter can come out and meet us all whenever she's ready. It won't be long, sweetheart."

Chastity blinked as her eyes filled with tears. "I'm so glad you're here, Mom."

"I wouldn't have missed it for anything," I said truthfully. There was a knock on the door and I grinned. "I'll go get that." My stomach was growling in anticipation already.

I love room service!

I rushed off to get the breakfast I'd ordered, finding a young waiter pushing a cart into the room. "Oh, thank you."

He nodded politely and left.

I poured myself a glass of orange juice, needing something cool and refreshing. "Chastity! Come eat, the hairdresser will be here soon."

The morning passed us by in a buzz of activity. The makeup artist did a good job with my makeup and the hairdresser did a lovely blow dry for me. I felt pampered and just a little beautiful, I had to admit. And Chastity looked absolutely amazing. Natural and ethereal like a goddess, with perfect, delicate flowers adorning her hair. "Oh, you look beautiful, sweetheart," I said, looking at her through the mirror she was facing.

Chastity smiled, her cheeks flushing a pretty shade of pink. "Thanks, Mom. So do you."

"It must be time to put your dress on?" I asked, standing up to rock the baby. My gorgeous Grayson was beginning to fuss again. He'd been such a little champion so far, but he was tired. "Your dad and the photographer will be here soon," I prompted, reminding her.

"Oh, you're right!" Chastity said, then got to her feet. "I might need your help getting it on, Mom."

"Oh, no problem," I said, taking Grayson out of the wrap and swaddling him up. My little angel was already falling asleep again. I tucked him in the portable bassinet the hotel had brought in for me and patted him on the back for a moment, making sure he was settled. Then it was time to help my daughter get into her wedding dress. My heart ached with the sheer beauty of the moment.

Chastity threw off her dressing gown dramatically, having a bit of fun with it, and pulled her gown over her head.

When it got stuck, I stepped forward to help her with the drawstrings at the back. I was struggling with all the emotions washing over me, so I coughed to clear my throat and tried to make a casual comment about her dress. "I'm glad you chose this type of closure. They're so much better than a zipper or buttons."

"Yeah, the dressmaker suggested it, actually, she said it was a good option since we really didn't know how big I was going to get."

I finished lacing her up and stood back.

Chastity turned toward the mirror to inspect her reflection.

"You look absolutely breathtaking," I managed to say, drinking in the sight of my gorgeous, glowing daughter. "You look like you've stepped right out of a fairy tale, Chastity."

"Thanks, Mom. This is really exciting, but I'm starting to feel super nervous."

Of course, she did. This was a big deal.

"What if he changes his mind?" Chastity suddenly whispered to me. "What if he realizes this is all a crazy mistake?"

I couldn't help but laugh. "Changes his mind? I don't think so! But if he did? He'd be officially crazy, and you wouldn't want him anyway."

There was a knock on the door, then Patrick walked into the room. "How's my family doing?" He looked toward our daughter. "Feeling nervous, sweetheart?"

She nodded and grimaced. "A little, but more in a *I hope he doesn't change his mind* kind of way. Not in an *I think I want to cancel* sort of way."

"Oh, he's most definitely not changing his mind." Patrick grinned. "He just about kicked me down the aisle to come get you. He's waiting by the metaphorical altar as we speak."

I picked up Chastity's colorful bouquet and handed it to her. It was time. My beautiful baby girl was about to take the next steps on the great pathway of her life, and I for one, couldn't wait to see where it took her!

CHAPTER 22

Kaiti / Katherine

Chastity's wedding was absolutely perfect. It couldn't have gone any more smoothly or beautifully. It was her dream come true, and the fact that she'd achieved it despite all the odds made my heart sing. The vows were sweet, heartfelt, and unique, while the venue was intimate and lavish. I spent the whole day sailing about in a cloud of happiness.

My daughter had found her happily ever after, and Patrick and I had found our way back to each other. It almost seemed like life couldn't be any more incredible.

After the speeches and laughter and all the deliciously rich food, Patrick kissed me and said, "I'm going to get a proper drink, I think."

I stood up, our baby still sleeping peacefully in the wrap. "Go spend some time with your friends. I'm going to go sit with Chastity and see how she's doing." I'd been watching her, and she seemed stressed or impatient. I wasn't sure which it was or why, but I intended to find out. We couldn't have the bride being perturbed on her wedding that was for damn certain!

Patrick nodded and headed off to chat with his gym buddies.

I walked over to sit beside Chastity at the bridal table. "Hey, baby," I said to her with a reassuring smile. "Are you enjoying your night?"

She nodded, then grimaced, rubbing her hands over her belly. "Oh…" she gasped.

I narrowed my eyes at her, noting the way she was holding her breath. "Hey. Are you okay?"

She relaxed suddenly, exhaling slowly. "Yeah, I'm fine. I'm just getting some cramping. It's probably from all the dancing."

At thirty-nine weeks pregnant? I don't think so, sweetheart!

"How long has this been going on?" I probed.

"Since dinner or a little after, maybe," She admitted.

I checked my cell phone and calculated the time. "So, three hours or so?"

Chastity nodded, blowing out her breath as though she were in pain once more.

I couldn't believe it, but I had to say it anyway. "I think you're in labor, Chastity."

"I was hoping it was just Braxton Hicks," she said, rubbing her big belly faster as if that alone might soothe my granddaughter wiggling up a storm inside her.

I nodded, remaining calm as Chastity seemed to be getting more agitated. "Well, most first labors take about twelve hours from start to finish, sometimes more, so there's no need to rush to the hospital. You just enjoy the rest of your party, and if you need to leave because it all becomes too much, tell me, and I'll smuggle you back to your room for a nice bath."

"A bath?" she asked, cocking her eyebrow at the suggestion.

"Or a shower," I added. "The hot water is great for pain relief. I spent most of your labor in a shower." And it was the main reason I'd even managed a natural labor with her. It had been a Godsend.

"Okay," she said, nodding and rocking on her chair in a way that screamed she was beginning to panic—which was completely normal.

I reached out a hand and squeezed her arm. "Just remember what I said. Don't fight the pain, it's doing something amazing. It's functional. Just ride the wave and make sure you rest in between every contraction. You'll need your strength for the last hour. Remember, labor is a marathon, not a sprint."

Chastity squeezed her eyes shut, grimacing in pain, before she exhaled slowly. "Yep. I can do this," she said, though she didn't sound entirely convinced.

"Of course, you can." I smiled at her. "You're one of the strongest people I know, and I'm so, so proud of you."

Chastity stared at me, her eyes opening wide as though she was surprised. "Thanks, Mom. I love you too."

I stayed with her, holding her hand and encouraging her to take little sips of water when she could. "You're doing *so* well, sweetheart. Just rest as much as you can in between contractions, okay? That is the key." I fed the baby and chatted casually with Chastity about how perfect the day had been, although I could see that she wasn't quite with me.

She was already fading away inside of herself to a safe place where she could find her strength and conserve her energy for what was to come.

Axel escaped the huge group of friends that had swarmed him and held him hostage for the past hour. He walked straight up to his new wife and smiled down at her. "Hey, beautiful. How are you doing?"

Chastity gripped her belly and smiled at her new husband. "We... I think I'm in labor."

Axel's shock was a palpable thing. "What?" he stammered.

"She's definitely in labor," I agreed calmly. "Contractions are every five to seven minutes. They're a bit irregular still, but they're getting stronger."

Axel hurried around the table and sat down next to her, his eyes imploring. "Why didn't you tell me earlier?"

I put my hand over my mouth to stop myself from laughing. He was panicked in a big way.

"Because I didn't want to leave yet. The first stages of labor can literally take hours. Plus, if it's a false start, we would have left our own wedding for nothing."

I was proud of how reasonable and calm Chastity was sounding.

Axel, not so much.

"Let's go *now* then," he urged. "Is it straight to the hospital? Or..."

"No. We have to call the doctor's service first to let them know we need her to meet us there. Plus, Dr. Martinez said to stay at home until I can't stand it anymore," she answered in between contractions.

"So, what do we do?" he asked.

I swallowed down the laugh that rose once more. Axel literally ran a multi-billion-dollar company, but confronted with his wife in labor, I could see the seams on his control splitting apart. "You could try a shower," I suggested. "Back at your room. Or maybe the hospital is the right place to be. Wherever you think you'll be more comfortable."

"Um... I think I want to go to the hospital, but I left my bag at home," she groaned softly.

I totally understood why she'd want to be in hospital. The safety element of being where you needed to go was comforting. "I'll get your father to pick it up for you. I've got to look after the baby. Hang on." I squeezed Chastity's shoulder, got up slowly with Grayson still asleep in his carrier, and went straight for Patrick.

He was standing among a gaggle of good-looking men. His gym friends, obviously. I didn't even look their way. "Sweetheart, I need your help."

Patrick set his glass of red wine down on the bar next to him and came straight through the center of the circle. "What do you need?" he asked.

I pulled him further away so we could speak a little more privately. "Chastity's in labor and needs her hospital bag, which she left at the house. How much wine have you had? Can you drive?" He could always take an Uber if need be.

"I haven't even finished that first glass," he said. "Let's go."

We weaved through the crowd, me following in his wake.

As we reached the bridal table, Chastity shot to her feet, a look of horror filling her face. "Oh, crap," she whispered. "That's *really* gross."

Patrick pulled his car keys out of his pocket. "Where's your hospital bag? I'll go get it."

"In our room," Chasity said. "Next to the bed. It's a pink suitcase, you can't miss it."

Then she looked at me and said, "Mom, my water just broke."

I couldn't help but grin at her. "Time for the hospital."

It won't be too long now.

"Axel?" Chastity called out.

"Yes!" he almost shouted. "Yes... car."

Patrick swung his keys around his finger. "I'm off to your house. I know where the spare key is. I'll see you at the hospital."

He slapped Axel on the shoulder. "It's go time, buddy."

Axel nodded and reached out for Chastity's hand.

Patrick dashed off, a man on a mission.

I walked beside my daughter, determined to support her in this crucial moment.

"Is your driver waiting somewhere around here, Axel?" I asked him as we slowly meandered toward the main doors. Patrick had already taken off, so I had to make sure these two actually made it to the hospital.

"Ah, yeah." Axel trembled as we stepped into the bright light of the foyer.

I stepped closer and grabbed hold of Chastity's other hand. "I'll walk with Chastity toward the entrance of the hotel. You get your driver to come so you can get to the hospital as soon as possible."

"Yeah. Okay," Axel said, nodding like a puppet, willing to step back from boss mode in favor of someone with more experience.

I laughed as Chastity and I shuffled toward the double doors like penguins dressed for a party. "He's really losing it," I remarked to lighten the mood.

Chastity managed to huff out a laugh too. "Yeah... funny, isn't it?"

"You mean the fact that the man handles more money and stress than anyone ever has... and yet one little contraction, and his brain blows up?"

Chastity giggled this time. "Yeah, something like that."

We soon arrived at the exit, and Chastity had to stop and breathe through another contraction.

I held her hands and stared at her beautiful face, feeling so grateful to be here for her in this moment. "I love you, sweetheart. You're going to do so great."

"Thanks, Mom," she said, just as Axel ran up.

"He's coming!" He announced. "Let's get you down these stairs."

I held Chastity's left hand and Axel held her right, and we managed to get her down the stairs safely and into the car waiting at the curb.

"I love you!" I called into the car window, at a loss for words. What else could I say in that moment?

"We'll call as soon as we can," Axel said, then he turned to the driver, and they took off.

I stood on the curb, watching them drive away into the night and toward the hospital.

Grayson stirred on my chest, lifting his little head, then headbutted my ribs.

I laughed and rubbed my hands along his back, soothing him with my love and presence. Life was truly perfect. In every way.

I'm going to be a grandmother soon!

I could scarcely believe it.

Epilogue
KAITI/KATHERINE

5 years later...

Grayson was a handful and a half. Even if I'd been twenty years younger, I doubt I would have been able to keep up with him! "I cannot wait until he goes to school in the new year," I said with a sigh.

He's like a tiny energy vampire!

Patrick laughed as he pulled off his shirt, displaying his gorgeous body to the whole world. Well... to me, and my dream kitchen, anyway. "You say that now, beautiful, but next year—mark my words—you're going to miss him."

"I still might go back to work," I said defensively, crossing my arms over my chest.

Patrick cackled as he walked off to have a quick shower, that criminally gorgeous ass disappearing from view.

"I might!" I yelled after him.

He didn't respond, but I could hear his laughter in my head. I'd meant to go back to work after Grayson turned one, but Patrick had convinced me to take an extra year to enjoy our son. Financially we were in a great place, and there was no real need for me to return. Or that was what Patrick had said.

Grayson would be our last baby, and truthfully, I wanted to see him grow and appreciate all the little things I missed out on when I had to return to work with Chastity. And Patrick loved having a wife that wasn't too stressed out and enjoyed cooking and maintaining the house.

And why wouldn't I. It's my dream home!

It wasn't the role I'd ever thought I'd play, but when I didn't have to work, my days opened up with countless possibilities. I had to pinch myself most days to remind myself that this was really my life. A loud crash in the playroom made me groan. "Grayson!"

Not again...

"I didn't mean it!" came his innocently childish response.

I took a moment to breathe, closing my eyes to keep my calm so that I didn't start yelling. That was the *old* Kaiti. I tried to maintain my cool as best I could these days. Becoming an older, second-time mother and new grandmother had taught me a thing or two about patience. I slowly made my way into the second living room which had quickly become a *very* messy playroom.

The Legos box was in pieces and colored blocks were strewn every-where, like a mini tornado had stormed through. "I didn't mean it, I promise!" Grayson grimaced, his brows raised hopefully to avoid a telling off.

His gorgeous little face made my heart ache in the best way. "I know," I said, as calmly as possible, but we didn't have time for this. "It's Maggie's birthday today, remember, so let's go get you ready, yeah?"

"Yes!" He jumped up and literally ran to his bedroom, zooming full speed like a little bolt of lightning.

We'd had Grayson's fifth birthday just a few weeks ago, which Chastity had missed because she'd been in labor, giving birth to Leo. Patrick and I had happily taken care of our other two grandbabies and had them stay with us for a few days while Chastity recovered. Although it had been *crazy* with the three kids all together; I'd had the best time of my life. I loved being a grandmother to such lively and spirited little angels. They kept me young!

Grayson rushed to get dressed.

With effort, I managed to get him into a nice pair of jeans and a blue shirt, though I was pretty damn sure he'd be covered in paint or glue or cake by the end of the day. This boy honestly ruined more clothes than any other child I'd ever met. It was almost comical and I'd long since given up getting upset over it. They were just clothes and thankfully we were in a position to afford more whenever the need arose. His happiness and development was our primary concern.

"I'm ready!" he sang triumphantly, as if it was him, and not me that just wrangled him into his cute outfit.

"Don't forget your card," I said, pointing at the table behind him.

"Oh, yeah!" he cried, dashing for the beautiful little card he'd demanded he be allowed to make during the week.

I knew Chastity would appreciate the handmade gift from her little brother more than anything else she could receive. "I'm going to get ready, now, and then we'll go, okay?" I told him.

He ran over and slid his tiny hand into mine. "Okay, Mom."

And there it was, the reason my heartbeat strongly every day.

We walked into the large living room—the one Grayson wasn't allowed to destroy—where Patrick, now dressed in tight blue jeans and a crisp white shirt, was waiting for us.

"Do you mind putting him in the car?" I asked. "I just need a minute."

"Of course," Patrick said, grabbing the car keys and holding out his hand. "Let's go, buddy." Patrick walked off toward the front door with our son.

I watched them go, my heart aching with joy.

My men.

Then I took a moment to go to the bathroom and do my makeup quickly. Gone were the days of spending hours on my hair and face. When you had to tear after a kid as full or energy as Grayson, you couldn't spare more than a few minutes. Thus far, I'd gotten my routine down to seven minutes, from start to finish. And honestly? I was happy with the results. Any more time these days would be a luxury!

I was walking out the door when I decided to head back inside quickly. I grabbed two bottles of wine. One for the party and one for me. When I got to the car, Patrick already had the music blaring.

Grayson was singing in the back like a little rock star.

My head ached and I wanted to open the bottle of wine in the car.

Patrick, ever in tune with my moods, slid a comforting hand over my thigh. "Ten-minute drive, that's all it is. Okay?"

I nodded and took a deep, calming breath. "Yep. Let's do it!"

Grayson chatted the *whole* way there. Ten minutes of non-stop, running commentary and a boat load of questions. He was the happiest and most inquisitive child, though he truly did my head in some days. As soon as we arrived, he began clamoring to get out of his car seat, eager to launch himself into the party like a firecracker.

"Wait," I said, though the child lock was on, and he couldn't get out without help anyway. I took my time getting out of the car. I was heavier than I'd ever been in my life, but Patrick didn't complain. Quite the opposite in fact. He threw money at me and told me to go buy new clothes to suit my shape and told me regularly that I was the sexiest woman alive.

I'd never even seen him so much as look at another woman since we'd gotten back together, and all my old insecurities were long dead.

"Let's go, beautiful," Patrick said to me, before helping Grayson out of the car and taking hold of his hand.

"Right behind you, husband!" I called playfully.

Patrick grinned and headed for Chastity's front door. Patrick and I had gotten married a year after Grayson was born. It had been small, intimate, and perfect.

We'd put a small fortune into landscaping our large backyard, and hired professional caterers, and enjoyed the reception at home. It had been lavish, but I'd also felt like it was money well spent when we'd improved the value of the property, too.

I walked up to the front door and pushed it open, still amazed that Chastity lived in this incredible house. Even five years later, her life *and* mine seemed surreal. I shut the front door behind me, hearing the kerfuffle my son was already making in the living room. As I walked into the large open space, I could see Maggie's birthday cake was front and center. A real princess castle cake, three tiers high with all the bells and whistles.

Perfect.

I wandered into the kitchen carrying the two bottles of white wine. "I know you can't drink, but I need one," I announced, setting them both on the kitchen counter. Chastity was breastfeeding, so wouldn't be drinking for another twelve months. Between her three pregnancies and all the breastfeeding, she hadn't had a drink in years. Six years, probably when I thought about it.

Chastity pulled out a glass from the cupboard. "Why? What's wrong, Mom?"

I slid onto the kitchen stool. "Oh, nothing, sweetheart. Grayson is the most healthy, energetic boy the pediatrician has ever seen. He has a perfect bill of health."

"Then why do you look like you just sucked on a lemon?" She opened the bottle of wine and poured me a generous glass.

I took a sip, feeling so old in that moment. Chastity had three kids and looked vibrant and alive. "Because I'm exhausted, hon. He runs me off my feet every day! I don't remember the meaning of 'sleep-in' anymore."

"He goes to school next year, so things will get easier," my daughter assured me.

"Yeah. Probably," I conceded. I drank some more, then glanced through the large windows to where my perfect little boy played. One day, I wouldn't be tired. One day, he'd be too old to hold my hand. But today I'd drink and complain; yet inside, I was still beyond grateful for everything I had, most especially my bouncy baby boy.

Patrick had gone back out to the car to get the present from the trunk and walked into the center of the room calling to our granddaughter. "Where's my little princess?"

"Here I am, Papa!" Maggie cried, waving her arms madly to draw attention to herself.

Patrick grinned at me and went off after her.

"She's surrounded by boys," Chastity said, nodding at Maggie with her brother, her uncle, and her grandfather.

I twisted on the stool and stared at the beautiful family picture they made together. "They're perfect. And speaking of perfect, where's my little lion?"

"Leo's in his bassinet," Chastity said, nodding in the direction of his room.

I hopped up and headed toward my newest grandchild, my wine forgotten. Leo was so delicious, and as soon as I stepped into his room and stared down at the newborn, my breath caught in my throat, and I was choked up with emotion all over again. "You are so beautiful, baby boy." I reached out and stroked his chubby cheek where he lay in his bassinet sleeping.

"How about we do the cake?" Chastity called out from the kitchen.

I couldn't stop myself from scooping the sleeping baby up into my arms. He smelled like divine perfection, and I immediately felt my ovaries aching. "Not a chance," I whispered to my temperamental hormones. I had three beautiful and healthy grandbabies to adore, plus two children of my own. I didn't need any more!.

I walked out of the nursery holding baby Leo in my arms and watched on, content and at peace.

Chastity organized all the kids around Maggie's amazing cake. "Ready? Happy birthday to you…"

As a family we sang while, filling the house with happiness and joy.

Maggie grinned at us all, lapping up the attention. Then after our three cheers and 'hip hip hoorays' she blew hard and extinguished all of her candles in one shot.

We all cheered, hoping her heart's desires would come true.

Patrick clapped loudly. He loved his little princess.

Meanwhile, the boys fussed to take turns at blowing out the candles.

"Okay, okay. Grayson's turn, then Thomas's turn, all right? Then we can cut the cake," Chastity said, wrangling them all like a pro. After all the kids had a turn blowing out the candles, she served the cake.

A little perturbed by the amount of spittle that likely covered the delicious confectionary, the adults sat out on the cat and allowed the children to enjoy it. Once they were finished devouring their body weight in sugar, we all sat outside on the deck to watch the kids playing under the tree and on the swings. It was a truly beautiful day.

I sat down next to my husband, with my tiny grandson in my arms and our big, crazy family running amok all around us. Our lives truly were the picture of happiness and together, we had our own little slice of suburban paradise. I was more content than I'd ever been, and I couldn't thank the universe enough for my second chance at love. With Patrick, Chastity, Grayson, Axel, Maggie, Thomas, and Leo... my heart was full, and my life?

Perfect.

THE END.

www.ingramcontent.com/pod-product-compliance
Lightning Source LLC
Chambersburg PA
CBHW060802210726
48292CB00013B/1724